I0678348

HALO DOLLY

AKA The Case of Grace

Rick Dewhurst

Quotidian Books

quotidian

Copyright © 2022 Rick Dewhurst

No part of this book may be reproduced, or stored in a retrieval system, or transmitted in any form or by any means, electronic, mechanical, photocopying, recording, or otherwise, without express written permission of the publisher.

ISBN-13: 978-1-7775730-2-7

ISBN-10: 1-7775730-2-5

Cover design by: Rachel Dewhurst

Printed in the United States of America

For Steve Taylor
(Only visiting this planet)

CHAPTER ONE

Okay, so this is how it all went down. I was looking for a wife. Sounds like trouble already, doesn't it? Well, you're right. I was headed for trouble right up to my private eyeballs, especially since I was destined to mix my emotions with taking on the devil's boys nose to nose.

Maybe you've never even heard of Spelunkers Global, that grimy horde lurking below ground, hell bent on undermining the human race. I'd been locked in a wrestling match with them for a few years now. And I wasn't the one who was winning.

As usual the game began with a case. You wouldn't believe how this case turned out even if I told you. Right now you wouldn't believe it, but after I tell you how it turned out you'll believe it, even though you'll find it hard to swallow. At the same time I hope you'll gain some understanding of how this whole world works. And it ain't pretty. But there is hope for us. So, stick around. You might learn something. I know I did.

The madness began one morning a few weeks ago. Christmas was coming, and it was cold outside. There I was, sitting in my big city detective's office in the penthouse suite of a big city building that was in a big city in the Pacific Northwest, a big city that was a lot like Seattle. I was comfortable here. Maybe too comfortable. I needed to get down to the gym more, but I'd stayed reasonably fit for a guy in his mid-thirties. My hair was still dark brown with playful curls and no gray. Blue eyes. An even six feet tall. Cute but sturdy. A sturdy, reliable type. That's what I was.

My Baby Boomer partners, Alfred and Abner, were passing the time bickering about the usual. And sure, I knew most PIs worth their salt worked alone, but God put the three of us together, so who was I to argue? Besides, they were company.

Alfred, a reformed hit-man, was aging well. Only a few lines of grey streaked his slicked-back, black hair. And despite a few extra pounds, he looked distinguished and durable in his black suit. Abner wasn't faring as well. Weathered now from years of alcohol abuse, his stubbly, red-leather face was topped by sandy-grey hair. Alfred and Abner had been competing for the same woman for a while now, but I'll save that story for another time.

There we were living in comfort at the top of our game. But as Providence would have it, that's when the Spelunkers saga began again. It was a soft beginning, hardly noticeable. It was their usual strategy. They would try to distract me with women, and then reality's hammer would strike.

The intercom buzzed. It was Penelope, my secretary and also one of my new step-sisters, but that too was another story.

"Yeah," I said.

"There's a sister here to see you."

"Which one?"

"What do you mean which one?"

"Brittany or Bertie?"

"No."

"No?"

"No."

"What then?"

"She's a Christian sister, not a step-sister."

"Okay. You win. What's her name?"

"You don't know her."

"Yes, I know, that's why, okay, fine, send her in."

Pen was in one of her moods.

Oh, man, who was this gliding into my office? Wow, did I ever have a good feeling about this. Alfred looked at her and then at me and sighed. Abner volunteered a muffled groan. I could feel their eyes piercing the side of my head, peering into my mind. But I didn't fault them for being jealous of my youth.

Alfred, the gentleman, stood, and I followed suit. Abner managed to push himself a few inches up from his chair. She seemed startled by the sight of three hardened detectives. I put her at ease.

"Have a seat," I said.

"Thank you," she said.

"What a knockout!" I thought out loud.

"Pardon," she said.

Abner and Alfred looked at me, eager to hear my reply.

"Sorry," I said, "I was just having a flashback of the fight last night, on ESPN."

"Do you get those often?" she said.

"No, yes, once in a while."

Abner picked up a magazine from the coffee table and pretended to read.

"I'm Grace," she said. "Grace Lane."

"Oh, I see," I said.

Alfred and Abner tried to look interested.

"So, you're our new assignment," I said.

"That's right. You're supposed to protect me."

"From what?" I said.

"What a question," Abner mumbled. "Maybe ya should take more useful night courses at that college, like courses about private eyein', instead of that useless writin' course?"

Unruffled, Grace said, "From what? Why from simply everything." And then she laughed.

So, she had a sense of humour. She was rich, and she had a sense of humor. Things were looking up. I'd never before seen anything that could compare.

And sure, I was taking a writing course now. I thought if I ever had the need to document a few of my more memorable cases, I'd have the knowhow.

Grace was fair, the way a woman could be fair when the blue of her eyes matched the gently lapping waves of a tropical sea, her hair crackling with yellow fire, her skin bursting with the healthy, athletic power of an Olympic gold medal downhill skier. She was about 5'7" and her....

"Are you alright?" she said, concerned.

Yeah," I said, "I'm alright. I was just thinking."

Yes, she was a woman for all seasons. Under her dark-brown, full-length, leather coat she wore a tight tan skirt that tugged your eyes on up to behold a full, fuzzy, taupe sweater that….

"Did ya hear that, Alfred?" Abner said, "Our boss and mentor was just thinkin'."

Alfred ignored him. So did I.

"What about?" Grace said.

"Security," I said.

"Oh, yes, that's good," she said, "and that's, of course, why I'm here."

"Well," Abner said, "now that we got that all straightened out."

"I'm Joe," I said, "and that's Alfred." Alfred nodded. "And, of course, Abner."

Abner forced a smile for everybody.

"That's us, Bell, Booker and Laflam, Christian detectives, we'll be taking good care of you, Miss Lane."

"Please, call me Grace," she said.

"Honored," I said.

"No problem, everybody calls me Grace, even the servants."

"Maybe we ought to get down to the details," Alfred said.

There he was, taking over. Alfred was forgetting again that I was the boss. Sure, he was older and knew the ropes and had been playing the game a lot longer than I had. But I was still the one paying the bills. Whatever. I decided to remain passive. I refused to fall into the trap of becoming resentful, which, left to fester, would lead to bitterness, with unforgiveness waiting in the wings for its chance to shuffle on stage and tap dance on my descent into hell. No, I wouldn't even sniff the bait.

"Yes," I said, "Alfred's right, let's get to the details."

There, I'd won. I was now bigger for the trial. I'd grown in Christian self-control.

"Of course I'm right," Alfred said.

He was pushing it now.

Abner added, "You'd do well to listen to us."

They'd succeeded in embarrassing me in front of Grace. I hoped they were happy now. I wasn't.

"So, who is in charge?" Grace said. "I naturally thought you were, Joe, since you are the one sitting behind the big desk."

Abner snickered, but I was glad she'd noticed.

"Yes, I'm in charge," I said. "I'm LaFlam. So who are we protecting you from?"

"Who?" she said. She tapped her pretty white fingers on my mahogany.

"Okay, whom," I said.

Grace, Alfred and Abner squinted their eyes and furrowed their brows.

"How's she supposed to know?" Abner said.

"Yes, I don't know really," Grace said. "Mother and Father are fearful, and without intending any disrespect to them, they're paranoid too. There were a few threats, nothing to be taken too seriously, all a big fuss for nothing."

She reached into her handbag and took out an envelope. She slid it across my big desk for me to take a look at. I nodded at Alfred and then at Abner before opening it. Grace knew who was boss.

I looked inside and pulled out three pages. I unfolded them. The message had been thrown together in the standard cut-and-paste-letters, a format popular in some extortion circles. And the message was clear. Grace was going to be dead meat. I looked at Grace and then at the paper. Some criminals had no class. To suggest the spectacular Grace would ever be anything dead was already a crime. To threaten so much life with lifelessness in the twitch of a trigger finger was too much grossness to be imagined. I blanked the image from my mind. There was no motive, either, other than the fact that her family was apparently heavily invested in the chemicals industry, and the parent company, in which they were majority stockholders, was polluting the entire planet, or so the misguided scum claimed. But why bump off a beauty such as Grace just because of that? Sometimes nothing made sense. And something else didn't make sense. There was no demand for money, or anything else. Only a threat.

Alfred got up and made the journey over to my desk. I passed him the letters.

"Nasty, aren't they," Grace said to me with a smile. Her eyes radiated warmth toward me, like when the leather seats in your Bentley began to pulse with the promise of a quick thaw to the morning cold.

"You said it," I said.

Alfred said, "Amateurs," and then handed the letters to Abner, who feigned disinterest, annoyed to be at the bottom of the shamus chain.

"It makes me feel so important," Grace said.

This was a smart babe, this Grace with the perfect frame, and she had no fear, none at all, and that scared me. And then I felt bad for calling her a babe in my mind. If she knew, what would she think of me? My mind, as usual, was a candidate for some needed discipline.

"You are important," I said and winked my cute left eye.

She winked back. This was going to be good. She was smart, brave, a true knockout and she winked back. I had to be dreaming.

"Ya, ya, we're all important," Abner said. "Only some of us are more important than others. Gettin' to pollute the planet and gettin' away with it, while the little people...."

"Okay," Alfred said, "let's get on with it. Who's been protecting you? You arrived here all by yourself."

"The last agency didn't meet my mother's strict requirements, so I'm briefly between protection right now. You, of course, are now taking over."

There was the rub. She had a mother. And by the sound of it, mother was one of those, the kind you had to deal with or be dealt with. There were mothers and then there were mothers. There was no happy time to be had with her kind. But nothing was perfect. I would persevere. Grace's returned wink guaranteed my follow through.

"Religious persuasion?" I said.

"Yes."

"Yes?"

"Yes, I'm persuaded." She winked again. I was shaken by her winking intensity. I tried to snap a tough, manly wink back at her, but my eye stuck shut, and then, as fortune would have it, so did the other one. In the dark, my lids strained to part, and then my eyes were suddenly released from their darkness, like window blinds loosed to jerk up on their roller. The scene was unbelievable. She sat there like Eve minus the apple habit. I made the decision. Protect her, court her, and then pop the question. At last I would be equally yoked.

"So," Abner said to Grace, "Who do ya think the anti-Christ is?"

"I've no idea," Grace said. "Is that important right now?"

"No," Alfred said, glowering at Abner, "It's not."

"They're pollutin' the planet, and next them multi-nationals will be persecutin' the righteous...."

"What," Alfred said to Abner, "have you been reading now?"

"Oh, good," Grace said, cheerfully, "we're going to do book reports."

This was a clever Eve. Nothing fazed her, nothing at all, not even Abner. I'd met my match. No, that was wishful thinking. I could see she was more than my match. Way more. But that didn't worry me. I didn't mind losing, as long as I won. Give a little to take a lot. There was nothing wrong with that, especially since slipping into the role of second banana came natural to me when it came to women. There was nothing I could do about it. She was her, and I was me. Some babes didn't mind if you were a little slower than they were; some even liked to mother you a bit, which normally I would have hated, but in this case nothing was out of the question. She was superior alright, and we were already winking. That was something I could take to the bank. With any success, I was going to be unequally yoked after all. Yoked to a superior babe. But I had to stop thinking of her as a babe. To think of her that way was a betrayal of Eve.

"I like the way you handle yourself," I said.

"I like the way you do, too," she said, and winked again.

So, we had an understanding. This was going to be good, real good, the way life could be good when life was going your way, when the scent of destiny filled the air, like jet exhaust from Air Force One. Then I remembered, and I winked back. I hoped she wasn't put off by my delay.

Abner said, "There must be a better way to make a livin'."

"Okay," Alfred said, "let's see what we've got."

There, he was taking over again. I decided to wait and see what he'd come up with before I let him know who was boss.

"What have we got?" I said.

"Ya, what?" Abner said.

"This is thrilling," Grace said.

"Okay," Alfred said again, "so we've got threats on her life."

"What do you mean, 'her' "Grace said. "I'm in

the room, I'm Grace, right here, remember?"

Nice going, I thought. She wasn't going to let Alfred bully her.

"Right," Alfred continued, "Threats by two-bit extortionists, who aren't extorting anything and they're lacking any sophistication whatever. And for this we're being hired to protect her...uh, I mean Grace, from harm. And what about the police? Did you inform them?"

"Yes, mother did," Grace said, "but they simply weren't that interested."

"Right, the police see the threats for what they are, and I presume your parents..."

"Mother."

"Yes, mother is the only one taking the threats seriously."

"Paranoid, as I said," Grace said.

"So, what do we have then?" I said.

"It's a put up job," Alfred said, "by your parents to make you think you're earning your own way in life. Easy money. Her mother, sorry again, Grace's mother, is fearful. She talks to your mother, presto, everyone's happy."

"But what if I'm killed?" Grace said.

Good for her, I thought again.

"And," Alfred decided to add, "I wouldn't be surprised if there wasn't some matchmaking scheme going on, also."

I liked this part of Alfred's speculation, and then I wondered if Grace could possibly be in on it, and then if she was, I then wondered if there was something lacking in her, some fault I couldn't see, appearances being deceiving, and all.

"Well," I said, recognizing the right time for me to take charge, "I don't care about useless theories. We've been hired for a job, and the job we will do. And we will get to the bottom of these threats also. She's safe in the hands of Bell, Booker and Laflam, especially Laflam."

"I'm in the room," Grace said.

"Right, sorry, Grace is safe in our capable hands."

"Are you finished?" Abner said. "If so, we need to have a schedule. You know, sayin' when it's our turn to keep an eye on her…I mean on Grace."

"Oh, good, who's first?" Grace said.

Abner added, "I would like to know fer how long we've been hired to do this job."

"Until I'm safe," Grace said.

"Don't worry, we'll crack this case," I said. "No problem there. And then you'll be safe permanently. Until then, you're safe in my hands."

I winked to seal the bargain.

"Just leave it up to me," I added.

Her eye only twitched.

I had a good feeling about all this, despite Alfred's scepticism. She was more than I could have ever dreamed or hoped for, and Christmas was coming too.

"Nobody's ever safe," Abner said.

CHAPTER TWO

On my way to the office the next morning, I began to think. Who was behind Spelunkers Global, anyway? Sure I knew about the rich folks. Not the ordinary rich folks, like me, but the real rich folks. The one per cent of the population who had 99 per cent of the wealth, the ones you didn't hear much about, the ones who were secretly running everything, from the media, to the government, to big tech and big Pharma. Or were they just conspiracy theories? One thing for sure, Spelunkers Global did exist. Their sinister activities were no conspiracy theory, except for the fact that people in the world didn't know anything about them, except for a few of us. My cell rang, interrupting my detective thoughts. I clicked on my hands-free calling, and braked in time to miss a bus pulling into traffic.

A gruff male voice said, "You need to meet me at the park on Little Mountain in twenty minutes. Come alone."

"Who is this?" I said.

"You'll find out soon enough. Meet me in the plaza across from the fountains."

"How will I recognize you?"

"Don't worry I'll do the recognizing."

I didn't like his tone. And it was also obvious

he was another one of those people who had control issues.

I had a lot to think about on my way to the park, but managed not to. I arrived in about 15 minutes and pulled into a parking stall in front of the fountains and cased the scene. Outside it was cold but not snowing. I looked across the plaza. It was empty of visitors, except for two men standing in front of one of the park benches. I guessed they were in their early-twenties, and they were clean looking, like two prowling Mormon suits on the hunt. What did I have to lose? I crossed the plaza to confront them. I wanted to get it over with, whatever there was to get over with.

"Okay, I'm here, "I said. "What's it about this time?"

The suit on the left spoke first.

"We're glad you asked, sir. I'm Elder McBain and this is Elder Smith. We would be happy to answer any questions you might have."

So they were Mormon missionaries.

"No, that's okay. My mistake. I was looking for somebody else. And, anyway, I've already been converted. I'm a Christian, but don't worry, I don't have anything against you and your mission. Live and let live. I would stay and talk it over with you, but I'm not a cult expert, and you might end up converting me. Besides I've got bigger fish to fry. I'm supposed to be meeting someone here who, no doubt, is a minion of Spelunkers Global. I'm sure you don't know anything about that nefarious group, and I don't have time to fill you in on that, either. Good day. By the way, you might get your higher-ups to buy you a couple of overcoats for this kind of weather."

I left them there in their youthful delusion, in the cold. At least I'd identified them correctly, even though I didn't know it at the time. I decided to circle the plaza on foot, waiting for the man behind the gruff voice to show his face. Where could he be? Half way around the plaza I heard it.

"LaFlam," the gruff voice said.

"Where are you," I said.

"I'm right behind you. Slow down."

I turned, and sure enough there he was, a man in his forties, wearing a navy, wool Pea Coat, a white turtle neck, black slacks, neatly creased, and a captain's hat. On his feet he wore white sneakers.

"Let's go over there to that bench where we can talk it over," he said.

I didn't know what we had to talk over, but I was going to find out.

The missionaries had moved off to save the world, and also do their part in bringing lost souls into servitude.

We sat down.

"So," I said, "What's it all about this time?"

"I'll ask the questions," he said, not unkindly.

"Okay, you ask the questions, if it makes you happy."

"I don't need your permission to ask questions. Besides, I don't have any questions to ask. I'm here to tell you a few things."

"So tell me a few things."

"I don't need your permission to tell you a few things, either."

We were at an impasse. I waited a few seconds and then asked, "What's with the white sneakers? You're looking pretty stylish, except for your choice of footwear."

"Don't get smart with me. I think you'll find out soon enough not to get smart with us."

So, he was now "us" and I knew who "us" was. "Us" was none other than Spelunkers Global.

I said, "I understand you're getting your thrills now by threatening to kill innocent young women."

"They got your attention, did they?"

"You might have simply dropped into the office and said hello instead. What do you mean, they?"

"That wasn't us."

"Why don't you just crawl back into the hole you crawled out of and leave the rest of us alone? And what do you mean that wasn't you?"

"It wasn't us. We don't threaten to kill people. We would just do it, if we wanted to. I called you because we need your help."

Sure, the oldest one in the book. Lure me in by dangling the carrot of need in front of me. And play on my compassion and pretend I was a person of value, and that I was a source of expert advice, a professional who had the skill to solve whatever dilemma they were facing. I'd heard it all before.

"How can I help," I said.

"Our leadership needs someone who knows

their way around. Someone who can negotiate their way through a minefield of deception. Someone who can retrieve the information we need and also survive."

"I've got no problem surviving. Nobody ever dies in my cases. Not yet anyway. But I don't think you've got a firm grasp on reality. I'm not going to work for Spelunkers Global, no matter how much you pay me."

"I'll say it again. We're not Spelunkers Global? I've been trying to tell you that, but you haven't been listening. I'm not one of them. In fact, we want you to help us uncover their operation, to bring them to the surface, so to speak. And we know you have extensive experience with that organization. And, of course, we will pay your standard agency fees."

"If you're not a Spelunker, who are you then?"

"I can't tell you that right now, except to assure you that we're members of the resistance."

So, he was a White Hat, one of the good guys, or so he said. But what did the good guys want with me? Naturally I wasn't forgetting there were good gals, too. There was good and then there was bad. Spelunkers Global were the worst of the worst. They were the bad guys, and, of course, I was not forgetting that in their organization there were bad gals, too.

"What are you staring at," he said.

"You might want to invest in a pair of sturdy boots. Black ones I think would best suit your outfit."

"Oh, I get it, you don't think I'm legitimate. You still think I'm one of them."

"I've seen this movie before. In fact, I've starred in it. You better come up with something fast to prove this isn't another one of those play-Joe-for-a-sap kind of deals."

He then reached into one of his breast, hand-warmer pockets and pulled out a piece of paper. He handed it to me. I read the contents.

"Okay, I'm in," I said and signed the non-disclosure agreement.

CHAPTER THREE

Abner and Alfred were waiting for me when I got to the office. They had that familiar impatient look pasted on their faces.

"So where have you been?" Abner wanted to know.

"I got a call this morning on my way here. The White Hats want me to help them get the goods on Spelunkers Global."

"Not again," Alfred said. "How many times are you going to fall for that same ruse?"

"Ya," Abner said, "aren't you gettin' tired of gettin' sucked in to playin' the same old game? And who are the White Hats, anyway?"

"You don't understand," I said.

"Oh, we understand all right," Alfred said.

"Ya, we understand," Abner added. "And we'll end up bein' the laughin' stock, as usual."

"Has this got anything to do with the threat on Grace's life?" Alfred said.

"Sure, they knew all about it," I said.

"Doesn't that tell you something?" Alfred said.

"It doesn't matter. I'm under orders from the top."

"From the top of what?" Abner said.

"I can't tell you. It's on a need to know basis."

"So," Alfred said, "do I understand this situation correctly? You're not going to let your partners know what's going on."

"I can't tell you right now, but you'll understand why later. You'll have to trust me on this one."

"I think I need a raise," Abner said. "If we're goin' to be operatin' blind, then I need extra compensation."

"Money's not the point," Alfred said. "Integrity is the point."

"Trust me or don't," I said. "But that's the way it is for now."

"Listen to our boss," Abner said. "Sounds tough, don't he?"

"Okay," Alfred said. "What's the next step?"

"We wait," I said.

"That's all we do is wait," Abner said. "We might as well just sit around and wait for the anti-Christ and be done with it. We're already in trouble. Ya know they've got those quantum computers now that hook up with the devil. They're like giant Ouija boards that get information from the other side. The same as they tried to do when they built the Tower of Babel. There's stuff God doesn't want us to know. And the demons are passin' that kind of stuff to evil folk who want to take over the world for the devil. They're hookin' up with that CERN portal, too. But who cares. I guess we're doomed anyway, so we might as well just sit around waitin'."

"Are you done," Alfred said.

"No, I ain't done. Google's got one of them computers and Amazon and Facebook, and they got all those algorithms workin' against us. The devil's got the whole world in his grip. And what I'm sayin' is all scriptural, too."

I said, "Let's hear about it later, Abner. There are a few things we need to consider right now."

I was surprised by the sound of my voice. I was sounding like I was in charge, like I was taking the leadership position, the one in control.

"You mean instead of just waitin'?"

"Okay," Alfred said. "Let's hear what we are supposed to be considering. What are our options?"

"Ya," Abner said. "What are our options? Maybe we need to get one of them quantum computers to figure them all out. Did you know that the guy who builds them grew up reading that occult storyteller H.P. Lovecraft. Lovecraft's the one who wrote those horror stories about gods and such. Demons, all of them. And now they're gettin' occult information from the other side."

Alfred said, "So then why would we want a demon computer, Abner? Try to make some sense, will you?"

"I am making sense. Spelunkers Global's got one of them quantum computers, too. You can bet on that. It's all about AI, and we don't stand a chance, no matter how much figurin' and considerin' we do, they'll be miles ahead of us."

I began thinking about our options while Alfred and Abner continued their bickering. We needed a ploy. That's what we needed. We were under orders from on high; there was no mistake about that. We were under orders to be active in taking down the most evil and corrupt organization the world had ever seen. Or in this case, the world hadn't seen the organization yet, because they were hidden, but when we exposed them, then the world in hindsight would see they were the most evil and corrupt organization ever. I decided it was time to interrupt Alfred and Abner's bickering.

I said, "We need to put our heads together and come up with a plan."

"Don't matter how many heads we put together, we ain't goin' to beat no quantum computer," Abner said.

"Would you stop the quantum computer nonsense," Alfred said. "If this is a battle of good against evil, then we have God on our side. Even if our esteemed leader keeps us in the dark about who's in charge of this show."

I liked Alfred's attitude. He was beginning to recognize who was in charge.

I said, "First we need to get in touch with Grace's mother, and fill her in about our thoughts on the seriousness of the threat, and see if she wants us to continue protection."

"What if we don't need to protect her no more?" Abner said. "What happens to your Romeo routine then?

Hmm. That presented a problem. I would then need to enter the murky waters of dating. How else would I be able to see her? And would she date me. And did people date these days? The sexes just kind of hung out now. Dating became dated after that TV show, Friends, hit the air. Well, I didn't want to be friends, I wanted to get married.

"Yer stuck now, ain't ya, Mr. Ladies Man."

"Drop it," Alfred said. "We need a plan."

That's right, "I said, "We need a plan."

"Why don't you first see if we're still in the protection business," Alfred said.

I succumbed and called the mother. She was terse. And emphatic. And where were we, she wanted to know? My view of the threat to her daughter didn't impress her at all. Grace was still our case, and I was blessed to know I could forgo dating for now. Alfred volunteered to take the first watch.

CHAPTER FOUR

Homegroup was gearing up for the night. We were washing down the sugar goodies with soda beverages. Next we would get down to the business of examining the purpose of our individual Christian walks. Our group had been studying a book that, if followed, pretty well guaranteed our entry into the company of the overcomers. We had all bought the book and the workbook that went with it. This was a new group for me in my new church, The Church of the Manifest Presence, and I'd only recently joined the homegroup. My initial reluctance to join centered around not wanting to get involved again. Going to church was one thing, developing relationships was another. Who needed the mess? On the other hand, caring support was needed if you were to survive in this sordid world, where wicked souls and demons salivated along the path you walked, horribly eager to tighten the trip rope and hurtle you headlong into their foul ditch of corruption. Or, for that matter, help was also needed if you just headed off the path all on your own initiative.

"Forty stinkin' bucks for the books," Abner said.

"Keep it down," I said.

Abner had felt a need for a group, and he

insisted we needed to be in the same group, since I was his mentor. I had countered that we already saw a lot of each other. He replied, sarcastically I thought, that we needed more quality time. Whatever his real reason, here we were, group mates.

"Commodification," he whispered.

"What?"

"Turnin' God into a commodity fer profit."

"What? Where'd you get that?"

"The '60s. Noam Chomsky, or somebody like that."

"That's not what's going on here."

"Why'd we have to buy the books then?"

"Not so loud."

I knew there had to be reasons for me to be tormented daily. Trials and testing were par for the spiritual course. But lately it seemed like I didn't have any clubs in my bag. But thank God for Grace. She had come into my life at the perfect time. She was my hope now. Of course, it went without saying that God was my first hope. He was my eternal hope. Grace was my earthly hope. But she wasn't second in my life, since she was in a different category. But overall, I had to admit that God was supposed to be first. And that was all there was to it.

The group settled into the living room chairs. There were eight of us. A good number for a group. I studied each in turn. Middle-aged Gus and his wife May, they were the hosts. They seemed nice enough. No power trips happening there. He was a machinist; she was a nurse. Fred and Ginger were the other couple. I didn't want to ask. They were retired. She'd been a teacher, he'd been a mill worker. The singles were Larry and Cynthia; everyone called her Cyn. I did want to ask, but played along since everyone else did. Larry, in his thirties, was a carpenter, currently unemployed. Cyn, in her mid-twenties, worked as a receptionist in a dentist's office. Abner and I rounded out the group. We were private eyes.

Gus asked May to open in prayer, which she did, competently, remembering at the end to thank God for the weather and the beauty of nature. No doubt she was a sensitive soul, who had caught the tail end of the counter culture movement. Gus then instructed us to open our books and workbooks to chapter 3. May then shot him a set of raised eyebrows.

"Oh, right," Gus said, "before we get started on our course, let's talk a bit about how our week went?"

"Our week went fine," Abner said. "Except maybe fer the fact we've taken on a case that smells like a setup from the word go."

"Okay," I said, patiently, "let's wait to see what happens, before we pass judgment."

"Yer dreamin', as usual," Abner said.

Cyn said, "My week went fine. It was exceptional really. I haven't had such an excellent week in some time."

"How so?" May said.

Gus gave wife May a sidelong glance.

"I got a raise. Praise God. And I bought a new vehicle, a Murano... "

"Murano, wow," Larry said. "Nissan. Good

choice. I'd like to have one of those myself."

"And," Cyn said, "I've got a new boy friend. He's a car salesman. I got a great deal on the Murano too. You know, payments I can afford."

Larry now looked less pleased.

"Well," Gus said, "Is he...?"

"Is he a Christian?" May said.

Gus turned his head again toward May, his co-leader, his face frozen in a cracked, frown-burdened smile.

"Well, we haven't gotten to that topic yet," Cyn said.

Gus hesitated, waiting for his wife's follow-up, but she shrugged and sat back in her chair. And then Gus realized he had nothing to say.

Ginger broke the silence.

"Fred and I had a so-so week. The usual. You know. Lunches at the Seniors' Center, and walks to and fro."

"We've got Netflix now," Fred said. "They've got all kinds of old movies. We saw a great one last night, didn't we dear?"

Ginger didn't answer.

"Which one?" Larry said.

"Napoleon Dynamite," Fred said. "It was made a few years ago. It's about this loser and his loser family. It's quirky, wouldn't you say, dear?"

"I didn't get it," Ginger said. "It was supposed to be funny, I think, but I didn't laugh once."

"How did you end up watching that?" I said.

"Grandkids' idea," Ginger said. "They laughed

like there was no tomorrow, and so did Fred. I didn't get it though."

"A couple of Mormons made it, I think," Fred offered as justification.

"Mormons?" Gus said. "Well, okay, Let's get down..."

"I saw it, when it came out a few years ago," Larry said, trying to help Fred out.

"Me too," Cyn said.

"Did you like it?" Larry said.

"Funny," Cyn said.

"Yeah, funny," Larry said, eager to agree.

Ginger said, "They don't make them the way they used to. Take musicals, they don't make many musicals these days."

"What about Chicago?" Fred said.

Ginger replied, "I said they don't make many. I didn't say they don't make any."

"Well," Gus said, "Let's..."

"I agree with Ginger," May said. "They don't make them the way they used to. Take One Flew Over the Cuckoos Nest, for instance. That was real acting. Jack Nicholson won the academy award for that, didn't he?"

"Can't remember," Ginger said.

"Me either," Fred said.

"I think he's demonized," Gus said.

"Who?" Ginger said.

"Nicholson," Gus said. "Nobody can act those parts like he does without some kind of help. Demons must be helping."

"Should we...?" I said, thinking we had lost focus.

"I agree, Joe," May said, "We shouldn't make snap judgments like that. It gives us Christians a bad name. Like we are judging everything and everybody all the time. And so what if Nicholson's got demons. He can be delivered. We should be praying for him, not criticizing. Besides, if acting was all about demons, then there would be more top of the line actors in Hollywood than there are now. He must have some talent. Can't be all demons."

"Hollywood's run by demons," Gus said.

May said, "See, those are the sweeping statements that get us labelled intolerant."

"We should be intolerant," Gus said.

"On The Waterfront, now that was a movie," Ginger said.

"Marlon Brando, wow," May said.

"He won an Academy Award for that, didn't he?" Ginger said.

"Can't remember," Fred said.

"Should have," May said.

"You should have taken care of me, Charlie," Fred said, in what was supposed to be Brando's voice.

We all stared at Fred. He grinned sheepishly and then yelled, "Stella."

"How's this all supposed to be helpin' our Christian walk?"

Abner said, impatiently. "I paid forty...."

"Culture's important," I said, cutting off Abner.

"This ain't culture we're talkin' about, it's

Hollywood."

Abner was right about movies dominating homegroup. I was beginning to wonder if I should be more forceful and intervene. I was a mature Christian, and I carried the responsibility for Abner's growth, which this line of discussion might stunt. Gus and May had lost control of their group, but they seemed to be enjoying it that way. I decided I was too new to the group to be taking over, and nobody had given me the authority to do that anyway. Gus and May had been appointed by the Church to lead. Who was I to interfere?

"Brando bought an atoll in the South Pacific," Gus said, "and he went to hell after that."

"Mutiny on The Bounty," May said. "Brando in a uniform."

Fred said, "The one they made with Charles Laughton as Captain Bligh was the best. Now there was an actor."

"He won the Academy Award for that, didn't he?" Ginger said.

"Can't remember," Fred said, and then added, "You'll hang by the yardarm," in what we assumed was Laughton's Bligh, issuing his last words to Fletcher Christian.

"I like some of the older movies, too," Cyn said. "Take Sin City, for example."

The group's eyes suddenly burned into Cyn. Gus and May gasped. Larry's indignation was betrayed by a grin.

"We shouldn't be watching those kinds of

movies," May said, and then she looked to Gus for support.

"No, of course not," Gus said.

"What's Sin City about?" Fred said.

"I don't think we want to know," Ginger said to her husband.

Suddenly courageous, Larry said, "I saw it too, on Netflix."

Cyn smiled at Larry, thankful for his support, and added, "I don't know what drew me to watch it."

"Backsliders," Abner mumbled.

"Casablanca," Fred said, changing the subject, "now there was a movie."

"Ingrid Bergman was so lovely," Ginger said.

"She won an academy award for that, didn't she?" May said.

"No," Ginger said, "she wasn't even nominated."

"Robbery," Fred said, "here's looking at you, kid."

"Lord of The Rings, was the best ever," Larry said.

"Wizards are demonic," Gus said.

"I have to agree," May said. "The scene where Gandalf is fighting Saruman reeks of occult power. Gives you the creeps."

"That's Christopher Lee playing Saruman," Ginger said. "I loved him in Dracula, I must admit."

"Tolkien was a Christian," Cyn said.

Larry smiled his appreciation to Cyn, who smiled back warmly.

"Debatable," Gus said, "besides, the makers of the movie weren't Christians, I'll wager."

"Gandalf was gay," May said.

"Only the actor, dear," Gus said.

"That's Gandalf the Gray," Larry said, "not gay."

"I don't know why I come," Abner said, frowning at me.

"Yes," May said, agreeing with Abner, "we really should get to the purpose for our group."

"Yes," Gus said. "We can't be sitting here all night talking about movies."

"Yer kiddin'," Abner said, "I thought that was the reason I was born-again."

Gus didn't know how to respond to Abner's sarcasm, so May took over.

"I feel we all need to repent," May said.

"What for?" Cyn said.

"Yeah, why?" Larry said.

"I don't see the need," Fred said.

"I'm not sure about that," Ginger said.

"Backsliders," Abner mumbled.

"I'm game," I said.

"Me too," Gus said.

"I think we all need to," May said.

"You can't make us," Cyn said. "If we aren't convicted of any sin, why should we repent?"

"Yeah, why?" Larry said.

May said, "We Christians always need to be repenting of one thing or another. None of us is perfect."

"You mean a general repentance?" Larry said,

"nothing to do with the movies."

Gus, taking the lead, spoke up, "For some of us it will be repenting for the movies, but for others, who for some reason don't think they've sinned by watching certain kinds of movies, they can examine their conscience, and then repent for whatever else they discover there."

"Amen," May said.

"I'm not so sure," Cyn said.

"Okay, then, maybe to begin with, we should take all of this to prayer," May said.

Ginger said, "At least we can all agree on that."

We bowed our heads. The room echoed the silence of introspection. I examined my conscience. There was nothing there. Yes, I was certain I didn't feel conviction for any of my movie-going habits. Sure, I'd seen a few, you know, iffy ones, but who hadn't? No, my conscience was good. I had nothing to repent for, unless…no, that wasn't anything. Everyone had those kinds of thoughts at one time or another, and if you had to repent every time you had one, that's all you would be doing, day after day, night after night. No, there was no sense opening up that can of worms. I blocked my mind from remembering. Into the sea of forgetfulness, that's where that kind of thought belonged. If it had to be dealt with, God would have to bring it up. If it was that important, He would. It was up to Him. Hmm. But if it was important, and it was up to me to do something about it, and God was waiting for me, then what was I supposed to do? Maybe God was speaking to me, and I just wasn't listening close enough. And how was I to find out which was right? Was God supposed to do it or me? Hmmm, maybe a fleece was in order, like, say, if Fred was the next one to say something, then I would have to look more closely at the issue, and then I would know that the time to deal with it had come.

"Excuse me," Fred said, whispering apologetically to May and Gus, "I have to use the washroom."

No, that wasn't right. That was a silly way to go about it. That was the trouble with fleeces; they weren't very mature. How could you ever really know for sure whether it was really God or only a coincidence? Or it might have been the devil who caused Fred to excuse himself just then. Although, the enemy wasn't supposed to be able to read your thoughts. Unless, of course, he instigated them, in which case the whole thing would have just been a setup, causing me to heap condemnation on myself, which, as every Christian knew, was one of the oldest tricks in the book.

My series of insights was interrupted by my pocket playing All You Need is Love. I answered despite the group's displeasure at my cell phone being left on. It was Alfred. Grace was gone. He'd blown his assignment. My happiness had been kidnapped. Homegroup time was over. I signaled to Abner we needed to go pronto. I had to get my future back.

CHAPTER FIVE

Abner and I sped through the city, the volumes of rain warring against us, my Bentley's tires sucking down hard on the pavement, the weather turning in on us, like the Moody Blues in concert. I wasn't depressed, only anxious. The news of my Grace being snatched from our hands rankled my pride, my private eye's pride, that is, and my heart sank to think that the two of us, Grace and I, might never be we. No, I wasn't depressed, only determined to get my Grace back. But my emotions needed to be capped right now. I couldn't let my personal feelings cloud my professional judgment. I needed to get out of the way and let my private eye gift kick in. That's the way gifts worked. They worked almost on their own. All you needed to do was let them fly, like Philip after he baptized the Ethiopian Eunuch. Where to start? That was the question. My private eye gift knew. Yes, first we had to talk to Alfred. He was staked out at Grace's family estate, and that's where we were headed.

"No, I'm not goin' to rub it in," Abner said to the rain that slobbered down his passenger window.

"I didn't say you were," I said.

"Ya, I know. It'd be way too easy to rub it in."

"Alfred is only human."

"Ya, we need to remember that," Abner said.

"But he'd rub it in if it was me."

I saw an opportunity to help Abner grow.

"Well, here's an opportunity for you to grow," I said. "Just ask God to help you keep from taking revenge."

"What do ya mean, revenge? That's not it."

"Sure it is, for the way he's always ridiculing you for your past."

"Oh, that don't mean nothin'. He's only on my case 'cause he knows yer Aunt Margaret likes me better. He thinks he's more of a success, having bin a successful hitman and all, and now he's so holier than thou that he thinks he's more spiritual than me."

I said, "He's always taking over too, and telling me how to run the business, but I'm not going to hold that against him. We're all growing together. We need to cut one another some slack."

"No, I'm not goin' to rub it in," Abner said again.

"And I'm his mentor," I said. "I can't hinder his growth by seeking revenge for my hurt pride."

"Ya, pride's a terrible thing. I'd have more of it, if I had somethin' to be proud of."

"Don't put yourself down. You've come a long way."

"Ya, and you're not so bad, either. Only deluded, that's all. No harm in that."

Abner was growing all right. He sounded almost caring, his usual sarcasm having given way to a hint of compassion. And under the circumstances, though I knew Christians were never supposed to be under the circumstances, I forgave him his remark about my alleged delusion. There was no need to correct him either. My record would speak for itself. When the score was tallied in the hereafter, my eternal reward would be according to what I deserved. There was no getting around the fact that it didn't matter what anyone else thought. But if people had a good opinion of you, that was fine. If you became well known for being a nice guy, that was okay. You might even become famous for being a great leader, or for saving the poor and downtrodden. Sure, fame was nice. But fame didn't count in the long run. Not that I would ever have any of it. That's not what I was striving for, though Christians weren't supposed to strive either. No, I was in the game to help others, and if a reward or two fell my way, such as a wife like Grace, and also recognition for a job well done, then I could justify taking up space on this crazy sphere of white and blue, orbiting the sun once a year, year after year, century after century, millennium after millennium, like an ageless greyhound chasing an eternal rabbit. But we all knew how it would all end. No, that wasn't quite right. Most people in the world didn't know, only Christians knew. No, that wasn't quite right. We Christians couldn't agree on how the world would all end, either. The Bible was pretty clear, but Christians couldn't agree on what the Bible meant. In fact, the Bible said that the world didn't end but..."

"Hey, turn here," Abner said.

I snapped back to driving and turned sharply, the rain in the headlights now flecked with snow. The temperature was dropping. I loved this time of year. I pulled up to the wrought-iron gate to the Lane estate and spoke my name to the intercom. The gate swung open and in we went.

"Yer fixin' to marry into this, ain't ya," Abner said, surveying the well-lit rolling lawn that led up to the mansion.

"That's not why I'm... "

"Sure, I know," Abner said, "It's love that makes the world go round."

"We've got to find Grace first."

"Sure, I know, yer smitten, and nothin' will be the same till ya find her."

"There it is, there's Alfred's vehicle."

"You can't miss it, can ya," Abner said.

Abner and I parked beside Alfred. He gave us a sidelong glance through the wet snow that was falling now. He was, no doubt, embarrassed and maybe injured. We sprang from my Bentley and jumped into his Hummer's back seat. I chose the back because I didn't want to face or embarrass him in his moment of weakness.

"Don't say it," Alfred said, staring straight ahead into the season's glory, the silent white flakes wafting down. Alfred was glum.

Abner said, "No sweat, it could have happened to any of us."

"Sure, rub it in," Alfred said.

"I wasn't," Abner said.

"Are you hurt?" I said.

"No, I was just not paying attention the way I

should have, that's all, since I didn't think there was any real threat anyway."

Abner said, "Got tired, did ya, well that's understandable."

I said, "Not your fault you nodded off. Why wouldn't you? You didn't think the threats were real, anyway."

Alfred said, "Grace's mother called the police. They're taking their time getting here. I decided to wait for you to arrive. Her mother is…"

"Is she a Christian?" I said, seeing a teachable moment.

"What?"

"You know, her mother, is she a Christian?"

"I think so."

"Well then, you'd better not say anything derogatory about her. We have to be careful not to make judgments."

"I wasn't going to judge her. I was going to say that she is terribly distraught. That's not derogatory, is it?"

"Not yer fault ya were asleep at the switch," Abner said. "As for me, I didn't think there was anythin' to the threats either. Could've happened to me, just as easy."

"What do you think, should we go in," I said, "and talk to the mother? Is she domineering, you know, the kind that controls everything, like a Jezebel type?"

Alfred stared at me in the rear view mirror.

Abner said, "No, don't worry about being

caught nappin', after all, Alfred, yer only human."

Headlights were coming up the driveway. The police had arrived.

"We'd better go in," I said.

The police were here. This was a real case now. But don't get me wrong. I wasn't objectifying lovely Grace in my mind by calling her a case. She wasn't just a case to me, but I knew that to the police that's what she would be. Just a case. But to me she was more, way more. But how could you explain that to hardened detectives, who only existed for the force? They thought blue and lived blue and had the blue so ingrained that they often led miserable, maladjusted lives, with the force becoming the only existence they know, as civilian life becomes more and more alien to them, and as their wives, or husbands, and the kids and the dog and the nosy neighbours fade into the daily humdrum of life. I was blessed to be only a private investigator. I still had feelings, which hadn't been smothered yet by the underbelly of society. An underbelly that overwhelmed your consciousness until you could see nothing but corrupted flesh. No, I wouldn't let that happen to me. I was too self-aware for that. I knew the score. I was passionate. I had a solid mind. I was a leader, too. Yes, I was an excellent example of what a Christian hardboiled detective was meant to be.

"On second thought," I said, "let's get out of here. If they need to talk to us, they can come and find us. We can come back and talk to Grace's parents tomorrow. I'll leave my car here."

There was silence. Then Abner said, "I think our leader finally made a sound decision. What do ya think, Alfred?"

"Let's go," Alfred said.

The police car pulled up, as Alfred started the engine and began to wheel us away. Abner waved and smiled at the detectives for effect, as we detectives, public and private, passed in the night, as the big, wet flakes, the size of flat, ornate golf balls, driven by the wind, sliced through the light cast by Alfred's accelerating stealth-gray Hummer. We exited through the gate, the white stuff flailing hard against the windshield, the silent wipers keeping time for no one.

"They're going to be annoyed," Alfred said.

"We can handle the fuzz," I said.

"Listen to him," Abner said, "he sounds like he knows what he's doin'."

"Thanks for the vote of confidence," I said.

Alfred said, "I really should have stayed and given a statement. I'm legitimate now. I don't have anything to hide."

"What do ya mean, legitimate? Yer fergettin' one thing, ain't ya," Abner said.

"Enlighten me."

"We're not legitimate, we're Christians. Did ya ferget?"

CHAPTER SIX

Back at the office we sat, waiting for the other shoe to drop. The party was getting rough. And that didn't cheer me at all. My spectacular Grace was now being man-handled by who knows who. Although, using the expression "man-handled" wasn't really correct these days. The criminals these days could just as easily be women, and in that case there was the possibility that she was being woman-handled right now, although thinking correctly ruined a perfectly good expression, since "woman-handled" sounded forced somehow. And what if both men and women stole my Grace? Then she might now be in the throes of being roughly used by both sexes, which would mean she was being person-handled, and that, of course, was so impersonal it conveyed no meaning at all. But however she was being handled, I wasn't happy, and we needed to do something pronto.

"We need to do something pronto," I said.

"I'm not convinced," Alfred said. "There's something that doesn't add up."

"Yeah, I get a strange feeling about it all," I said.

"Strange, what's strange?" Abner said. "Ya mean it's strange that the three of us are here in the detective business, an ex-hitman, an ex-drunk and an ex whatever ya were? Uhh, ya weren't anythin' before, were ya?"

I ignored Abner's shot. I hoped if I ignored him long enough, my trial would finally be over, and he would start to be kind to me all on his own.

"No, Abner, if you say so," I said. "Let's not go into it, shall we? And by the way, you're not an ex-drunk, you're an ex substance abuser."

"Thanks for cheerin' me up," Abner said.

"I wonder why it all seems so strange," I said.

"Did ya hear that, Alfred? Our leader keeps thinkin' it's strange. If you want to hear strange, I'll tell ya again what's strange, in case ya didn't get it the first time. They got that CERN machine over there in Europe? A collider, they call it. They're plannin' to open up a portal so the demons can come through from their dimension and bring along with them some dark matter that'll drive everyone nuts. The world's done for."

"Thank you for that update," Alfred said. "And if you really need to know, I was mostly praying, and then I must have nodded off."

I exchanged glances with Abner.

"Shoulda been praying harder, don't ya think?" Abner said.

I said, "That's crossing the line, Abner."

"Okay," Abner said, "but what are we goin' to do?

I shook my head at Abner.

"Okay, sure, alright," Abner said. "I'm sorry, Alfred. But what are we goin' to do? Just sit here?"

I waited for Alfred to answer. Alfred wasn't

answering, and he looked like he wasn't going to answer. He was maddening sometimes. When you didn't want him to take charge, he usually did, but when you needed his input because you were fresh out of ideas, he would clam up.

"Any ideas?" Alfred said to me.

"No," I said. I remained calm. He wasn't going to upset me this time.

Alfred said, "Grace's gone, and you don't have any ideas?"

"No," I said again. "I'm waiting for my private-eye gift to kick in."

Alfred and Abner stared at me. Then Alfred snickered and Abner followed with a chuckle. Neither said a word. Meanwhile, I would remain firm and wait for my private-eye gift to kick in. When the gift kicked in I knew I would have plenty of ideas. The important thing I had to try to remember was that gifts were all about timing. Timing was one of the most important attributes of gifts. They worked on their own time. Sometimes when you tried to force them they wouldn't respond, and at other times they had to get your attention to get you moving. You didn't want to run ahead or fall behind. You wanted to be in perfect timing. Sometimes, at times like these, I fell into the pit of doubt. Was my gift that strong? Was my private-eye gift strong enough to justify my chosen calling? No, I hated to think that way, and I wouldn't think that way now. I had resolved for about a year now to ignore any doubts that might try to creep in about my sleuthing ability and simply stand on faith.

Remembering this, I waited patiently for my private-eye gift to prompt my mind to give me the words to speak. While I was waiting, I began to reflect on my way of thinking, the way I spoke to myself and to nobody. And a fear was growing inside me. I wasn't sure where its roots were, but I suspected that if I found the fear and its roots I would lose my identity. I would lose my private-detective way of thinking, and I might even begin to think the way everyone else did. Normally. And I would no longer be me. I would then only be your average Joe. No, I had to hold on. My way of looking at the world was my way, and sure the going could get tough, but I was born to be tough, the way a man was supposed to be tough in America, sleuthing in the naked city in the heartland of the American Dream. But still I wasn't fooled by the dream. I wasn't going to strive to achieve. I had my priorities. I knew by now that the little things were the things that counted. Sure you could chase after the big bucks, and you could chase after the big reputation and the glory, and you could chase after the big girls...or whatever...and you would never get where you needed to go. Yes, the little things were where it was at. Like the pleasure of driving your Bentley down the street in winter, and smiling at the common people on the sidewalk, or having a sudden insight into the corruption of the human condition, or revelling in the unique splash of flavor from a Quarter Pounder, as the combination of onions, cheese and beef dropped softly onto your tongue and then rose gently to tease your palette.

"Why don't we drive over to McDonald's and have a hamburger and fries," I said, the words rolling off my tongue.

"That's yer answer?" Abner said, "burgers?"

"Okay," Alfred said, "here's what we need to do."

There he was, taking over again. I decided to wait to hear what he had to say before reasserting my authority.

"What?" I said, not unkindly.

"We need to go back and see the Lanes tonight. And then tomorrow we need to take another look at those threatening letters, and then nose around and find out what environmental groups are the most militant, the ones who would be the most likely to try something like this."

I decided now was the time to put my foot down. Alfred wasn't going to bully me. "Yeah, but let's go get burgers first."

Alfred frowned.

I said, "Okay, why don't we just go through the drive thru."

CHAPTER SEVEN

Eight cylinders rumbled their pleasure to the black rubber ruggedly hugging the white sparkling city streets, which frigidly whispered winter is here to the guts of the sleek, gliding stealth-gray Hummer. Alfred sternly gripped the wheel. I rode shotgun. Abner lounged in the back, nursing his chocolate shake. Empty wrappers and bags were all that remained of our meal, except for the abiding smell of spent burgers. Alfred, health-conscious ever since he dodged the heart-attack bullet, had said no to the grub. He couldn't eat salad while he was driving, he said. And he did insist on driving. Yes, the temperature was going down, and so would those selfish, inconsiderate felons who stole Grace. I had no doubt about that. Yes, the winter outside was frightful. The snow was now the size of salt, peppering the windshield. We were headed back to see the Lanes. The men in blue had probably left by now. I wondered if the Lanes would let us in at this time of night, stolen daughter or not, but we had to try. Yes, and what was it all about really? Sure Grace was missing, but she'd been missing from my life up until now anyway. I heard my last thought, and it hit me hard. I was becoming more calloused. The detective business changed a man alright. But I had to maintain my positive view of life. Where would I end up if I fell for the dark view, the "everyone's doomed" view? I stared unblinking through the Hummer windows at the city, the white city in winter, the city that endured no matter what the people or the weather threw at it, and I knew I would never go down that road, the one that led to the Dunkin' Donuts of lost hopes and forgotten dreams, where for a dream and six bucks you could buy a Vanilla Bean Coolatta and a place to lose yourself. But as for finding Grace, I had no worries. She was the wife for me, and I sure wouldn't let us down. And besides, nobody ever died in my cases anyway.

"Ain't ya a bit ashamed of drivin' this gas guzzlin' monster?" Abner said. "And ya wonder why Grace gets kidnapped, her family bein' involved in pollutin' the planet and all."

Ignoring Abner, Alfred said, "I wouldn't be surprised if the Spelunkers were tied up in this somehow."

"What do you mean?" I said. "The guy I met from the Resistance said they were."

Alfred didn't answer.

"Can't ya smell the setup?" Abner said. "AI's got the whole thing planned. They're way ahead of ya. There's demons everywhere, runnin' the show."

I sensed that Alfred and Abner weren't eager to stay the course. They thought it was the same old trap, but they didn't know what I knew. I was one step ahead of them this time. I knew who was leading the Resistance. The King of the White Hats himself.

But I couldn't tell them. Non-disclosure meant just that, non-disclosure. And now I wasn't the only one fighting against that scum. The Spelunkers were at the bottom of everything evil on terra firma, and I needed to follow the trail, no matter where it led, even to the depths of hell, and now I had company. In fact, if we had to go there, the Resistance would be leading the descent. It wouldn't be like the last time, when I lost big time. The Spelunkers played me and made me look like a sucker, setting me up for that Super Duper reality show. But that was another story. And it was bad. I looked bad, real bad, and when one detective looks bad, it's bad for detectives everywhere. It was my fault, and I wanted to erase the whole episode from my conscience, although I hadn't let on to anybody that it was on my conscience. No, I wouldn't give anyone the satisfaction. They had won, but I'd won too. I'd kept my positive attitude, although the whole demoralizing mess, when I thought about it, ate away at me. That's the way it was with a positive attitude. Your attitude sometimes failed, and you again fell into the kind of fear of failure that upset your positive applecart. And when it began to eat away at me, I wanted to get those Spelunkers real bad. But revenge was bad. There was no end to it. The Spelunkers got me, and I would get them back, and on and on it would go. No, I had to be the mature one. I had to be the one to turn the other cheek. I had broken the mould of tit-for-tat, but this time they were going down hard and for good. Although right now I didn't want to think anymore about them. I had other fish to fry.

"I'm not afraid of Spelunkers, or their demons" I said.

"You ought to be," Alfred said.

Abner sucked hard on the milk shake dregs for effect, and then said, "When the end comes, it's the end."

"It's Christmas time," I said, "why do you have to be so negative?"

"I ain't done my shoppin' yet. And, by the way, are we havin' a staff party or ain't we?"

I knew Abner was being intentionally irritating. And why not? He knew he was good at it. He'd hit a nerve this time though, with the whole subject of etiquette and gift-giving, and what was appropriate for different occasions. I didn't have a clue. Should I have a staff party? Should I get Grace something, if we found her? What was the right thing to do? Aunt Margaret, my former mother, she was easy. Just get her something that smelled good. But now that I had a lot of dough, were the expectations higher, and what was I to get my new, real mother, and my new dad, who had more than they would ever need? But the whole family issue was another story. There was no sense in thinking about it now. And what do you get a guy who drives a Hummer? I loved Christmas, but not the confusion it brought with it. There was no question, gift-giving was hard.

Outside, in a doorway, a solitary street person crouched against the cold. A lost soul. You didn't have to be a poet to die in the gutter.

"Those were the days," Abner said.

CHAPTER EIGHT

Mrs. Lane let us in. The hired help must have been in bed for the night. And why was she smiling? She wasn't just glad to see us. I knew then the case was about to take a turn. And sure enough, there she was. There was Grace in front of the gas fireplace, smiling too. The rich were tricky, I knew that much. Of course, I was rich now too, but I wasn't so tricky as those with the old money. I was only a Johnny-come-lately with new money, or at least it was new to me. Yes, I knew there were two kinds of people in this world. There were those poor suckers in the old days who had to get the videos back to the store on time, and those who thought it was optional. And the poor suckers always covered for the careless. It was the same way for the haves and the have nots. The have-nots covered the haves with their labor, with the sweat of their brow, while the haves just sat back and watched the movie, and when it was done, the have-nots had to remember to get the movie back to the store, as they labored to keep their lives and their world together.

But what had happened? Grace was here and happy. That fact led my deducing mind to an inescapable conclusion. I would have to get her a Christmas present. If we'd got her back after Christmas, I would have been spared the trip to the mall. Then I noticed it again. My callousness. Where had my love gone?

The three of them now stood there in front of the fire, the gas fire, where no labor had ever been needed, no wood carried in, no ashes carried out, only warmth produced. They posed, lord and lady of the manor, poor rich people, much to be pitied, with their daughter Grace, their hope for the future. And she was my hope, too. At least we had that much in common.

Abner spoke first, "So," he said to Alfred, "it didn't matter that ya fell asleep on the job."

Grace escaped from her parental tableaux and rushed toward me, "They simply let me go," she said.

She was darling. My callousness turned to putty. I could never objectify her? I could never think of her as just a case? Love began to stir in me once more, as the details of the case faded into the background.

"Who let you go?" Alfred said, getting down to the details.

"There were two of them," Grace said, "both men, I think, but I didn't get a good look at them."

"No," Mr. Lane said, "she didn't get a good look at them."

"Certainly not," Mrs. Lane said. "We are oh-so happy to have her back. I would have never forgiven myself if anything had happened to my dear Grace."

"Unforgiveness is unhealthy," I said. "It can lead to severe illness, such as arthritis, and can even kill you eventually."

Alfred frowned at me.

"He's right," Abner said, "unforgiveness nearly killed me. If I hadn't repented, I'd still be drunk in an alley abusin' myself."

Mr. Lane cleared his throat.

"I'm so blessed," Grace said, "to have been spared."

She had that right. Now I was blessed too, and I wasn't going to let her out of my sight again, except, of course, when it was Alfred's or Abner's turn to protect her.

"Okay," Alfred said. "Let's get this straight. There were two of them, and you can't give us any idea as to their identity, except you think they were both male."

"Correct," Grace said.

"And where did they take you?" Alfred said.

"It was dark," Grace said, "and they put a blindfold on me and tied my hands, and they said they had a gun. We rode in a car, and then we stopped, and then we went into a building of some sort because it got warmer and then they sat me on a chair or sofa or something. It smelled like French Vanilla."

I said, "The upholstery smelled like French Vanilla?"

"Or maybe just the air in the room," she said.

"Do you know why they let you go?" Alfred said.

"Not really."

"Then," Alfred said, "you mean you might have some idea?"

There was Alfred taking over again, doing all

the interrogating. But I had to forgive him. He did it out of an honest and sincere heart.

"Well," Grace said, "another person came into the room and there was some shuffling, like they were in a panic, and then one of them untied my hands. Then there was more shuffling and then a door slammed and there was silence."

"Did anyone say anything?" Alfred said.

"I only heard a few words before they rushed out."

"And?"

"It was a male voice. I heard initials and muffled words. He said SG, and then I heard him say something like there was someone in SG who wasn't going to be happy."

"I knew it," I said. "It's Spelunkers Global."

Alfred raised his eyebrows at me.

"Then, when it was quiet for a while, I took off the blindfold and I was in a dingy room, the sofa I was sitting on was filthy."

"Oh, dear," Mrs. Lane said.

"And the French Vanilla," Grace said, "was no longer in the air."

"How do you know it was French Vanilla?" I said.

"Discernment," Grace said.

"We know our vanilla," Mrs. Lane said.

"It's getting late," Mr. Lane said. "Perhaps the questioning could continue at a later time."

"Just to add," Grace said, "in case you wanted to know. The room was in a warehouse. I think it was at the corner of Victoria Street and Marine Drive. They didn't take my cell phone, so I called a cab, and, well, here I am."

Yes, there she was in all her glory. What a peach! My admiration was interrupted by the chiming doorbell. I knew it. We would have to face the music. There was no getting around it. In they came. The men in blue had come back. But they weren't wearing blue of course because they were detectives. Mrs. Lane showed them in, and we dispensed with the pleasantries in jig time. The first flatfoot, the older one, was heavy-set, his tan trench coat sloppy, his coat sleeve the victim of a recent cold, his tie askew. His yes-man was short, thin and had the bearing of a weasel in winter, minus the nice coat. The heavy-set one gave us the long once over. His yes-man followed suit.

"These are detectives Bannon and Smart," Mrs. Lane said, breaking the ice. "And these are Grace's security people, private detectives Bell, Booker and Laflam."

"You boys know anything about this?" Bannon said.

"What?" I said.

"You were supposed to be providing security, weren't you?"

I didn't like his question's suggestive tone, and I knew Alfred didn't. Bannon continued with his attitude.

He said to Grace, "So you said on the phone they just let you go."

Grace said, "That's right detective."

"It's really getting late," Mrs. Lane said.

"Just a few more questions," Bannon said.

I decided to help them out.

"There were two of them," I said. "It was dark, she was blindfold, her hands tied, probably packing heat, took her for a ride, into a building, air smelled like French Vanilla. Somebody else came in a panic, and then they just left her there."

I intentionally left out the part about Spelunkers Global. That was our exclusive information. After all, we were the ones who knew what SG meant.

"Are you finished?" Bannon said.

"Nice summary," Grace said to me.

"Anything to add?" Bannon said to Grace.

"No, that's about it," she said.

"Who was guarding her when she was kidnapped?" He looked at me. "Was that you?"

Alfred stepped into the fray.

"I was," Alfred said.

"You see anyone, or hear anything?"

"Not a thing," Abner said, sticking up for Alfred, "he was sleepin'."

I was going to correct Abner and say he was praying, but Alfred glared at me, and I let it drop.

"Okay," Bannon said to Grace, "your parents already said earlier they don't know who would want to harm you. How about you, any ideas?"

"Pollutin' the planet," Abner mumbled.

"What's that?" Bannon said.

"Nothing, detective," I said. "He's just up too late."

"No," Grace said, "I'm an innocent victim, who has never done anyone any harm."

That was good. I liked her style. We were going to get along real good, the way people get along when their vibrations are twanging at the same frequency. She smiled at me and then winked. I could almost read her thoughts, or at least I thought I almost could. But then did you want to read the thoughts of others? No, you probably didn't want to know. You didn't really want to know what others thought of you. No, reading the minds of others would be a bad thing this side of heaven. Of course if there was only love in the world it might work, but we were a long way from total love on this planet. No, knowing the thoughts of others on this crazy mixed up world would kill you, and fast. But on the other hand, maybe it would work for two people, like Grace and me. No, not likely, but there was nothing to worry about because knowing the thoughts of others just wasn't going to happen. And even if you could know their thoughts, the other person wouldn't admit it, anyway.

The men in blue left and we followed them out, but not before Grace and I exchanged departing winks. Outside, I beeped her open. I was happy to be back in my own car.

CHAPTER NINE

The next morning before going to the office I stopped off at Starbucks for a matcha latté. I needed time to think. The usual crowd had gathered to covet their caffeine before facing the day. I found a vacant soft chair in a grouping of three. I ignored the other two patrons who ignored me back. No need to converse. It was an unwritten law. Alienation was the order of the day.

I sipped and thought. There was something strange about the kidnapping. Sure, I knew all kidnapping was kind of strange, when you thought about it. Stealing a person, for one reason or another was strange. But this one had a smell about it that came from only one direction, and that direction was down. I don't mean it was an earthy smell. I mean it was a smell more like fertilizer. And that smell came from only one source. Sure, I knew the smell of fertilizer might come from a farmer's field, but that's not the source I'm talking about. Not this brand of fertilizer. This brand was coming from none other than Spelunkers Global. I was sure of it. And Grace told us she heard the letters SG. And I had filled in the rest. SG stood for none other than Spelunkers Global. Now the question to be answered was why were they faking a kidnapping? And was I going to ask questions and then answer them myself? Yes I was. And why were they faking the kidnapping of my client? Because they were trying to lure me in again, that's why. But why? Odds were that they wanted to use me for something again. They needed a fall guy to take the rap. That was the answer. But the rap for what? What did they want to lure me into this time? But they were in for a surprise. What they didn't know was that the White Hats were part of the program now, and they wanted to use me for something, too, something I hoped would lead to the Spelunkers' downfall, or in this case their up-fall, when they came up to be exposed for all the world to see.

So the game was on. And whatever version of the game it turned out they were playing, I knew I was going to be in jeopardy sooner or later. And would I make it out alive? Yes, I would, because nobody ever died in my cases. At least nobody had so far. But I knew there was always that chance. And even though I had only recently discovered my real family, I was sure, like most people, that I had come from a long line of people who had died. No, you could never count death out.

I checked my phone, finished my latté, nodded to the heads buried in their apps, exited the caffeine den, and headed for the office, where I hoped to gain more clarity with the help of Alfred and Abner, or at least from Alfred. I needed his input, just as long as he didn't try to take over. Like most people, he had control issues. But not me. My control wasn't illegitimate control, since I was the boss and the rightful person to be in control. And so what if Alfred and Abner didn't recognize my authority most of the time,? That was their problem, not mine.

CHAPTER TEN

At the office, there they were, sitting in their usual chairs. I walked in as Abner was giving Alfred a lesson about the atmosphere.

"Chemtrails," Abner said. "It's those chemtrails."

"They're contrails," Alfred said. "They're just jet exhaust."

They looked up at me and nodded. Abner resumed.

"Contrails don't hang up there all day spreading out till the sky's hazy and blockin' the sun. Haven't ya ever looked up?"

"Of course I have. They're contrails."

"Do ya know what's in 'em? There's chemicals, like Barium and Aluminum. But that's not the real problem with 'em."

"Tell me," Alfred said. "I can't wait to hear about your latest find on the Internet."

"Nanobots."

"Nanobots?"

"Yep, they're dropping nanobots on us. We ingest them, and they stay in our bodies for good. Everybody in the world is filled with 'em. They're gonna hook us all up to the cell phone network. Then we'll all be controlled by AI and the Draco Reptilians."

"Reptilians?" Alfred said.

"Yep, that's what they call the off-worlders in charge of the planet. But they're really just demons. They got most of the New Agers fooled into thinkin' they're from other planets. Some of 'em live underground. They got big cities full of 'em down there. They're probably the ones in charge of the Spelunkers. They got a huge base in Antarctica, too, in the huge caves under the ice."

Abner's insights about the Reptilians living underground got my attention. What if they were the ones responsible for the Spelunkers? It made sense, in a nonsensical way.

I said, "Why didn't you mention this before about the Reptilian demons, living underground. It might have been helpful."

"Okay, that's it for me," Alfred said. "Maybe it would be helpful instead for us to focus on Grace's case."

"Sure," Abner said. "But you'd think fer most people in the world, such as you, that the first thing they'd want to find out is what's goin' on and what they're supposed to be doin' here on earth. Most everybody's asleep to what's really happenin'. You need to take the red pill, so ya can see."

"I can see just fine," Alfred said. "And since I'm now a Christian, all the fundamental questions have been answered. And I have been forgiven."

Alfred was solid. He had withstood the test of time. Yes, time was a big test, and we were all taking it. And Alfred had done better than most, despite his former occupation. The consensus was that killing people for a living was a bad initial career choice.

"Suit yerself," Abner said. "But when that Tesla guy wires ya up with a neural mesh to link ya with AI and the global net, don't come complainin' to me. And ya also aughta know that the elite er plannin' to mix their human parts with technology so they can live forever. They call it transhumanism. It ain't gonna work though. Ya can't transfer people's souls into plastic and metal parts that are all stuck together and expect a good result. Besides, God ain't goin' to go fer it, neither."

"Okay, thanks once more for your insightful summary," Alfred said. "But I guess the first thing we need to know is whether the Lanes want us to continue protecting Grace. Have you considered inquiring about that?"

He was talking to me.

"I suppose I was just assuming they weren't in need of our services any longer."

"Assuming?" Alfred said.

"All right, I'll find out."

I wasn't looking forward to talking to Mom, but before I could call her on my cell, the intercom buzzed.

"She's here." Pen said.

"Who?"

"That sister."

"Okay, okay, send whoever it is in."

"Sure, whatever you say. It's your life."

"Grace floated in, an angel without wings,

filling my life with purpose and my heart with joy. ..."

"Yer thinkin' out loud again," Abner said. "I told ya, that writing course yer takin' is affectin' yer mind. Airy, fairy literature don't belong in the private eye business."

"Smooth talker," Grace said to me.

I rose from my chair to greet her and impetuously took the lead.

"Care to go for coffee?" I said.

"Delighted," Grace said.

Alfred said, "So does this mean we are, or we aren't, in charge of your security?"

"Ya," Abner said. "I gotta know 'cause I'm studying the Book of Revelations and I want to get back to it..."

"It's the Book of Revelation," Alfred said, "not Revelations. There's no 's' on the end."

"Ya, sure, Mr. know-it-all. Okay, so if we're not needin' to protect her...I mean her ladyship, Grace Lane, I wanna get back to my studyin'. I'm just getting' to the good parts, where the whole evil scheme of the Harlot and that Beast Babylon is exposed and they get what's comin' to them. Especially those crooked traders who exploit the poor and leave their trails of pollution all over the planet."

"I'm not responsible, Abner, for what my Father has been doing," Grace said, graciously.

"That's right," Alfred said, "leave her alone. She's just a victim."

"I'm not a victim, either, Alfred, and for your information I am no longer in need of your protection, although mother isn't in total agreement with that decision."

Well said, I thought.

I could see now the future opening up for me, like a ripe melon. The future was the sun and I would glory in its passionate embrace, for better or worse. The road would be long, the rewards great, the two of us travelling as one, deflecting the slings and arrows of life's cruel journey, from birth to death and onward into eternity.

"Okay, then I'm outta here," Abner said.

"So am I," Alfred said.

"And so am I," I said.

"And so are we," Grace said and winked.

I winked back. My winker was getting stronger.

For effect, Abner said to me, "Yer mission, should you decide to accept it, is to try to please her for the next fifty some-odd years."

"Thank you, Abner, for that insight," I said.

Grace and I took the elevator down. Abner and Alfred chose to wait. We left them there, waiting for the elevator to return, their Baby Boomer fatness slipping away, as grey lines slithered through their thinning hair, stalking them like subtle serpents.

I watched the floors blink downward toward my destiny. Yes, I was blessed, or what I meant to say is that I thought I was about to be blessed. Or could you be blessed when the blessing hadn't happened yet? I mean, could you just claim the blessing as yours, before it happened? And was that scriptural? If you claimed the blessing before it actually happened, such as marrying Grace, for instance, then you would be saying that you were making it happen somehow. Would you then be able to create your own reality? But if you could create your own reality, then wouldn't you be like God? If so, there was something really wrong with that idea. But if you claimed the blessing, anyway, and if what you wanted to happen, didn't happen, then what? There were those who would say if you didn't get what you wanted, then you just didn't have enough faith. And there was something really wrong with that, too.

Grace was beside me going down. I hoped she wasn't seeing my knees shaking.

CHAPTER ELEVEN

We landed in the parking garage, my manhood shooting strength to my knees. I had to be brave. Facing the Spelunkers was nothing compared to the terror of wooing a wife, a life partner who would be there for you through thick and thin, the good times and the bad. But we were off to a good start, since Grace didn't seem needy. And that, at least, was one of us. The elevator ride had been pretty cosy. She smelled good, too.

I beeped my Bentley, and opened the passenger door for Grace. That's when I heard it. The gruff voice. It was coming from the Mercedes beside us.

"Hold it," he said. "We've got some business to talk over. Get in the back seat. She can come, too."

"Am I being kidnapped again?" Grace said. "What fun! And this time we can be kidnapped together."

I was impressed by her courage, a wife for all seasons.

"Shall we?" she said to me.

I was then struck with a stray question that flitted through my mind. Actually they came as a pair, flying tandem. Could Grace possibly be a White Hat? Or might she be a Spelunker Queen? She was a Lane, after all, and her family was intimate with the corrupt

RICK DEWHURST

elite. Either way I was one woman short of a full bridal party. Although if it turned out that she was only a White Hat, then maybe she wasn't just stringing me along, and I still had a chance. Another possibility was that she might just be her. I liked that proposition the best.

We climbed in and waited.

"We're going for a little ride," he said.

He was sitting in the front passenger seat. I didn't like the looks of the goon behind the wheel. His dull eyes glanced back past my head as he shifted into reverse. I could see he'd faced some opposition in his life. One cheek had become close friends with his flattened nose. He backed up and then wheeled us out of the garage

"Did you buy those boots I recommended?" I said to gruff.

"Always the smart guy," gruff said. "But carry on. That trait of yours might come in handy before long."

"Oh, thrilling, we're going for a ride," Grace said.

I didn't share Grace's optimism. I knew I was about to come one step closer to the inevitable. A confrontation with the Spelunkers. I didn't have a real problem with confrontation. I just did my best to avoid it.

"Do you mind if I call you Gruff?" I said.

"What do you mean, Gruff? Are you trying to be amusing again?"

"I think it's because of your voice," Grace said,

covering for me.

This was getting good. I could see us making an excellent team, in addition to being romantically involved. Although sometimes those kinds of relationships ended in disaster. Time would tell.

"My name's Leopold. You can just call me Leo."

"You can call me Joe," I said.

"I'm Grace," she said. "Isn't this fun?"

"This is serious business," Leo said. "We're about to take down the most sinister cabal the world has ever seen."

"Aren't we actually going to take them up?" I said. "And technically, the world hasn't seen them yet to compare them with any other evil villains we've seen in history."

Flat nose snorted and Leo grunted.

"Where are we going?" Grace said. "I need to tell my parents. They worry. But of course I'm not worried, because I'm with you Joe."

Her warmth spilled over onto my insecurity and bolstered my resolve.

"We can't tell you where we're going," Leo said. "But you'll be safe. We have a meeting to attend."

"What kind of meeting?" I said.

"Call it a strategy meeting," Leo said.

The plot was unfolding. I knew that somehow I was going to be the main event in their plan to expose the underground. I was used to that by now. But this time Grace was with me. I hoped she'd be along to see me succeed, whatever the plan was, and she would see how important I was to the future of the world, as we knew it. I didn't mean that in a proud way, of course. Pride was the enemy of the Christian walk. In fact, pride was the enemy of anybody's walk, whether they were saved or unsaved. The bonus for being a Christian was not needing to pay the price for past sins. You could just repent and be done with it. But if you weren't saved, you were in danger of taking your arrogant pride-walk straight down to hell. It would be easy going, and there would be some fun along the way, but the landing wasn't pretty. No, hell wasn't a good subject to bring up with the lost, although calling them lost wasn't well received, either. There was no getting around it, the whole idea of hell annoyed people.

Grace popped her seat belt and moved a little closer to me. What a comfort it was to have a Christian sister along for the ride.

"Nice Mercedes," she said and smiled, her white teeth gleaming.

"You two cool it back there," Leo said. "We don't have time for that now. You need to concentrate, Joe. No distractions."

"I'm hardly a distraction, Leo," Grace said. "Think of me as more of a permanent fixture."

Man, did I like the sound of that, unless, of course, she was playing me for a sucker. I did have to admit to myself that I was suspicious. She had come on to me strong after only a few days. And I knew I wasn't that desirable. Or maybe I was. I didn't want to sell myself short. Love at first sight worked that way, or they wouldn't have called it love at first sight.

After about ten minutes, Flat Nose pulled the Mercedes into a parking garage and stopped in a stall. He stayed with the limo while Leo led the way to an elevator. Inside he punched the top floor, and we headed up.

"Nice boots," I said to Leo. He didn't respond.

The smell of Grace hadn't faded. I steadied myself for what lay ahead and prayed for success.

"Are you praying, Joe," Grace said.

I nodded.

"So am I," she said.

We needed all the help we could get, and where was the best place to get it? From the Boss, of course. When you were travelling in this earth realm, if you weren't packing some heat, then it was a good idea to pack some glory for protection.

The elevator stopped. The top floor was one suite. A guard at the entrance frisked me. I was clean. Grace stared him down. We could see a group of about five people sitting in armchairs. They were leaning forward, their heads together, discussing something. Leo directed us to join them. They were expecting us and welcomed us to sit. I took the lead and boldly found a chair. I wanted to impress Grace. Then I remembered and stood to wait for Grace to sit. Then I sat, too. She didn't look impressed. In fact she didn't seem to care one way or another about my attempt at chivalry.

"So what brings us here?" I said, smiling at Grace. She winked.

Three of them were military. Two men and one

woman. The other two were civilians, one man and one woman, both dressed in casual business attire. Leo returned to the door and stood with the guard. His new boots squeaked.

The gray haired army General spoke for the group.

"We're Q," he said.

A lot of people wanted to know who Q was, and now here I was in the midst of one of the greatest conspiracy quagmires of this century. Most thought there was no Q, but here they were right in front of me. It was a red letter day for me.

"Leo gave me your letter," I said. "I complied with the ND. I didn't even tell my suspicious partners who it was that wanted to hire me."

"You mean five people are one letter?" Grace said. "How ingenious."

"We're not hiring you," the General said. "This is on a volunteer basis, as a way to serve your country and save the world. There can be no price tag on that. You will, of course, receive your standard agency fees for your services. But should we succeed, and succeed we must, the eventual book deal alone will compensate you sufficiently."

He was right. I was the world's servant. I didn't need the money anyway. I was set for life. But I had a question. Not long after Leo had let me know who wanted my services, suspicion had begun to creep its way into my mind. Was Leo really from Q, and did Q even exist, and if there was a Q, did he represent the real Q? I wouldn't be a PI worth his salt if I wasn't on my toes at all times. Alfred and Abner would probably have accused me of being too gullible and too impetuous when I agreed to sign on. I was thankful that the ND had saved me from their abusive questioning. I was confident now that my PI gift was intact and I was in the right place. But still I needed to ask the question.

"I've got a question," I said.

"Shoot," the General said.

"How do I know that you're Q and that you're the genuine White Hats hell-bent on destroying the Spelunkers and all that's evil in the world?"

"You don't," he said.

"Fair enough," I said.

"I don't know anything about Q and White Hats and conspiracies," Grace said, "But these seem like nice people. And I'm pretty discerning when it comes to first impressions, as you well know, Joe."

My heart skipped a beat. I wondered if that was a good thing.

"That seals the deal for me," I said, and winked at Grace. She blushed.

"Okay, fine," the General said. "Now that we've got that settled, we can proceed."

"Is this going to be fun, or what?" Grace said.

"You'll need to sign a non-disclosure agreement too, young lady," the General said.

"Ooh, I love keeping secrets," she said.

The Admiral spoke up. "Now that we have finished with the Q&A, can we get on with it?" she said. "This operation is time sensitive, as you know.

And Q+ needs to receive a report on our progress."

The General nodded.

The Admiral didn't seem like a control freak. She was military, and the military had to be in charge. And she was Navy, and if the captain wasn't in control of the ship, she would go down. No, she wasn't a Jezebel type. She was only doing her duty.

The rest of the meeting was heavy. They told me the part I was to play. As it turned out, I was more than just a cog in the wheel of fortune that would ultimately land the world on the winning wedge, or condemn humanity into bankrupt lives controlled by the evil elites bent on world domination. I wasn't just a cog, I was the whole game. Grace was impressed.

The briefing ended, and Leo led us out and down in the elevator. Grace was pensive. She had a lot to think about after our meeting with Q. She would have questions, especially since she had never before heard about Q. Most of the world hadn't. Of course the media called Q only a conspiracy theory, but what did they know? Then there were those of us who knew the score and could be counted on to save the world according to Q.

"That was informative," Grace said. "You mean to say that Q has been telling us on the Internet what is going to happen, before it happens?"

"Yes," I said. "He, uh, they, uh, Q posted it all in code. You had to decipher the code to know what he, uh, they, uh, Q was telling us."

"All in code?" she said.

"Yes, you had to figure it out. The posts were

like Q tips for those who had ears to hear."

"Fascinating," Grace said. "So now we're going to help Q come true."

"Exactly," I said. "But as you just heard, we can't rush this. Timing is everything."

Leo seemed bored with us.

"Parking garage. All out," he said. "I'll drive you to your car."

CHAPTER TWELVE

The next morning I was back at the office. I had a lot to think about, and Abner and Alfred would be of no help. How could they be? They knew nothing about the hazardous journey I was destined to take.

"So what is next on our PI plate," Alfred said.

"Ya, are we goin' to just sit around here all day," Abner added. "And I take it yer girlfriend don't need no more takin' care of, since it looks like yer goin' to take over that job permanent like."

I wasn't in the mood to spar with either of them this morning. The fate of the world was at stake. Not that Christians were supposed to believe in fate. Fate was pushed by the devil for suckers who didn't know the score, for those who needed a way to explain the dismal results of their efforts on this planet. No, I knew who was in final control of this planet, and it wasn't the devil. The devil was on the losing end of this game. Not that life was a game, it was more like a trial, and you passed or you failed, depending on who your attorney was. And, of course, God was the judge. But still the evil in our day on this earth went deep. I had suspected it went deep but I didn't know how deep, until yesterday when Q dropped the dime on the devil. The truth was that the Spelunkers were only surface bait, and the devil himself was their benefactor. I reviewed the part I was to play and shuddered.

"Are ya cold?" Abner said. "Ya need to get that girlfriend of yers over to warm ya up."

"Leave him alone," Alfred said. "He looks like he's got enough on his mind."

"Ya, and he won't tell us anythin' about it, neither. And we're his partners, and not only that we're supposed to be his Christian brothers, too. And he gives us the silent treatment."

"I can't tell you the truth right now, Abner, or I would."

"Truth, what is truth?" Abner said. "I don't hear it much from so-called believers. Why don't Christians ever tell the truth to one another? Christians 'er supposed to, ain't they? But there's this excuse they all give about grace or somethin'. Accordin' to my scripture readin', we're supposed to tell the truth in love. But nobody really loves nobody enough to tell them the truth, so nobody says nothin' about sin. But the thing Christians are real good at is takin' offence."

"Thanks for that, Abner," Alfred said. "Meanwhile, I've got a hunch the devil has got a hold of Joe's tongue."

So there was Alfred fishing for information. He was subtle, too subtle for a former hit-man. Well, I wasn't going to fall into his trap and spill the beans.

"The devil hasn't got my tongue, but he's got just about everything else in this world," I said.

"You don't plan on taking him on directly, do

you?" Alfred said.

Why did Alfred always need to pry? And what was I supposed to say now?

"They been lyin' to us for centuries," Abner said. "It's demons runnin' the show."

I was relieved that Abner had unintentionally come to my rescue.

"I know I shouldn't ask," Alfred said, "but how are the demons running the show?"

"Easy, they got dupes in every country. They're called politicians. And some of 'em are actual demons wearin' people suits. Some of the crazy conspiracy folk think they're aliens. And others think they're a race of Reptilians who are born here and live among us. But they ain't aliens or Reptilians. They're just demons, minions of Old Slewfoot himself. And then there's the clones..."

"Okay, let's stop there," Alfred said. "I'm dying to hear about the clones, but we've got other business to attend to."

"Like what?" Abner said.

"Yes," I said, "like what?"

"I don't know why I have to explain it to you," Alfred said, "but just because we aren't protecting Grace anymore, doesn't mean we shouldn't be trying to find out who was behind her kidnapping, even though it appeared to be a fake kidnapping? Kidnappings aren't fake, even if they have a happy ending."

Alfred had a point. Of course, I knew who was behind the kidnapping, and so did Alfred, and so did

Abner. But I needed to keep them busy while I fulfilled my part in Q's plan. I needed to keep them from discovering the real mission I was on. They needed to be protected from the truth.

"Sure, we need to follow up," I said. "Why don't you two take charge of that? I have a few other things to take care of."

"He's losin' interest, don't ya think?" Abner said to Alfred. "Could it be that somethin' else is occupyin' his mind? Somethin' to do with our last client?"

"Maybe it has to do with what he won't tell us," Alfred said. "How about it? What's really going on?"

I needed to keep them from interfering in Q's plan, so I decided to agree with Abner.

"Okay," I said. "Grace and I are hitting it off really well and we need some time to get more deeply acquainted."

"Ooh," Abner said. "More deeply acquainted, he says. Aren't ya getting' eloquent? Maybe those writin' lessons are payin' off for ya, Mr. Don Juan."

Alfred didn't look convinced, but he took the bait anyway, pretending he believed my story.

"Alright," he said. "We'll handle the rest. Take all the time you want getting acquainted. Abner and I need to earn our keep, anyway. Oh, and also, by the way, whatever you're not telling us will come to light in the end."

Alfred's words were prophetic, whether he knew it or not. That's what happened sometimes. People sometimes said things, and it turned out that they were right and what they said actually happened.

In this case, one way or another it was true that everything was going to come to light in the end.

Sunday was coming, and I decided to ask Grace if she would come to my church with me. I hadn't been attending this church for long. I knew that church hopping was not recommended, but everybody did it these days. But really I wasn't church hopping. I had only attended one other church in my life. But my old one was more conservative than this new one. The Church of the Manifest Presence was called a charismatic church. The gifts of the Spirit were operating there, and there were some who were prophesying in order to edify the body. One Elder was especially prophetic. His prophecies were poetic. He prophesied in limericks. I'd only been going to the church for a few months now, but I was already on the verge of despising prophecy.

CHAPTER THIRTEEN

Sunday came around, like the earth ceaselessly rotating, all of humanity waiting for the day when peace would come. But there would be no peace until the Prince of Peace returned. Until then we would continue to meet on Sundays and pray for relief from life's torments. Although, there were some religious folk who decried meeting on Sundays. They were Sabbath people. They met on Saturdays, the rightful Sabbath, they claimed. The Emperor Constantine was the culprit they said. He was responsible for making peace with the pagans and combining their festivals with Christian festivals, which initially came from Judaism, since they were the first followers of the Messiah. But the modern day Jewish followers met on Saturday, too, which might have seemed confusing unless you knew the history. And most didn't, including me. Some of the results of all this controversy were Halloween and Santa Claus and Easter bunnies. But who didn't like a good scare once in a while, and presents at Christmas, and Easter eggs and good times, except when Uncle Earl had too much to drink and the elephants in the rooms of North America shrieked "dysfunctional" from their trumpeting trunks?

"Where are you?" Grace whispered into my

ear. "Are you meditating on the Word your Pastor is giving?"

I couldn't tell a lie, especially in church on Sunday, even if it was true that we weren't supposed to be meeting on Sunday. Of course I wasn't supposed to lie on Saturday, either, or on any other day, for that matter.

"Ya, what are ya thinkin' about," Abner whispered. "Your secret mission, or somethin'?"

Abner and Alfred had insisted on sitting with us. Abner seemed to think it was great fun to take on the role of chaperone.

"Would you stop whispering?" Alfred said, "I'm trying to hear…"

"You're whisperin', too," Abner said, "if ya haven't noticed."

I squeezed Grace's hand, and she knew. She knew I was lost. Yes, I was lost in my thoughts and in the exquisite atmosphere of her presence. Pastor Bernard's Christmas message was adequate, what I heard of it. He was a good pastor. He cared. He wasn't just a hired hand.

"Amen, brother," Abner yelled for effect, as Pastor Bernard's sermon ended.

The worship team began to play O Come, All Ye Faithful, but was interrupted by the prophetic Elder, who had a prophetic word for us:

"You need to admit you're a sinner,

before you can live like a winner.

But when the going gets tough, you know God is enough,

And make sure you pray before dinner."

That one wasn't bad, I thought.

"Good word, brother," the Elder's wife said.

"Prophecy needs to be judged," Bernard said, "So does anyone have any discernment on this one?"

No one responded, and I couldn't help but think that The Church of The Manifest Presence was a few stones short of a full church.

After the Benediction the congregation was dismissed, and most of us headed for the coffee pot and snacks in the foyer. The redeemed gathered in groups to have fellowship. I wondered if the groups were the same every week. How could you get to know more than a few people anyway in a church of a couple of hundred? Of course, that's what the homegroups were for. For closer intimacy they called it. But who wanted to get intimate with a group of Christians? There was something unseemly about it. But there was no doubt that I wanted to get intimate, and she was standing right there beside me. I was enjoying the fact that I actually had a woman with me at church on Sunday, and then Abner disturbed my thoughts.

"How many of these people would still be here if there was real persecution?" he said.

"Seriously, Abner?" I said. "Is that all you can think of to speculate on?"

"That's okay, Abner," Grace said. "It is a relevant question."

Hmm, that was a first. She'd contradicted me in front of my partners. Was this a sign of things to come? We tie the knot, and suddenly she is the one in charge. Oh, well, worse things could happen.

"I'm sorry to contradict you, Joe," she said, capturing me with her eyes, "I know you are living under great stress, given the mission you have agreed to undertake."

I was happy she was apologizing, but I knew then that our lives together would inevitably be those of give and take. That's what made the world go around. Still, I didn't like her using the word "undertake," and I didn't like her talking about my mission in front of Alfred and Abner. Why did male-female relationship have to be so difficult? And we hadn't even engaged in any real intimacy yet. And of course we each would have needs we expected the other to satisfy. Yes, the world was full of needy people. And life was a full time job. But I was thankful that time would inevitably be consumed by the timelessness of eternity.

"Tell us about your secret mission," Alfred said. "Are you out to save the world again?"

Abner snickered. "We're goin' to end up wearin' it, as usual. And this time we don't even get to play the game."

"I get to play," Grace said. "I'm part of the plan. But I can't tell you anything about it, either. I signed an agreement of non-disclosure."

"Who with?" Alfred said.

"Ya, who with?" Abner said.

"I think we need to be on our way," I said. "And don't forget Christmas is coming. We need to celebrate. Who knows when Christmas will come again?"

"It comes every year," Abner said.

CHAPTER FOURTEEN

After church Grace and I sped through the wonder of winter on our way to the Lane estate. We were approaching her gate when my cell rang. I beeped on my hands-free calling and swerved just in time to miss an errant black feline.

"The end is near," said the strident male voice.

"Yes, I'm almost home," Grace said, having been aroused from a post-service, peaceful meditation. "But you don't have to yell."

"Who's this," I said.

"I'm Grace, of course, silly."

"No, on the phone."

"You really don't want to know," the voice said, "but I'll tell you. We're your worst nightmare. And you know what that means. And you know who we are."

"He's not very nice, is he?" Grace said. "Perhaps you should hang up."

"We know who you are, too, Missy, and you're not going to get away, either."

I pulled my Bentley up to the Lane's gate and stopped.

"You don't scare me," I said.

"Well, I'm a little worried," Grace said. "And that voice...I recognize that voice...I know, he's one of those kidnappers."

"Figures," I said, not knowing why it did.

"Listen, the two of you. We know who you've been talking to, and their plan isn't going to work. We're way ahead of you. We told you not to do it, but you're going to anyway, aren't you, LaFlam?"

"Have you got one of those quantum computers?" I said.

"Never mind that now. We're going to give you a chance to bow out of this whole game and then you and your lady friend won't get hurt. Otherwise, you're dead meat."

"Nobody ever dies in my cases," I said. "At least not yet."

"There's always the first time, and in fact I guarantee it."

"Okay, so what can I do for you? We haven't got all day. Our lunch is waiting."

"Listen smart guy. I already gave you your options. Back off means you stay alive. Go forward with the plan and you're dead. We've improved on the Chronovisor now. Before we could only use it to see into the past. Now we can see into the future, too. You make the wrong decision and you're dead, and that means both of you. We've seen it."

"What's a Chronovisor?" Grace said.

"Who knows?" I said. "We can ask Abner later."

"By the way," I said to the voice. "Did you happen to notice in that future seeing device if Grace and I get married, and how many kids we have, that sort of thing?"

"Oh, don't be silly," Grace said.

"Yeah, don't be silly, Joe," the voice said. "You've got more things to worry about than that."

So here we were, in the middle of a quantum computer game of chess. And we were the pawns. AI was playing us all for suckers, and even this Spelunkers Global guy with the bad attitude was a victim. I needed to remember that. He was a pawn, too, and I needed to develop compassion for all people, even the worst of them. After all, the worst of them were headed for destruction. And what made matters worse, you couldn't really tell who was who without a scorecard.

"Have you seen yourself in hell?" I said. "Not a pretty picture, is it?"

"Still the smart guy, eh? Okay, just to let you know what's going on, go have a look in your trunk, and I'll get back to you when you've come to your senses."

"He beeped me off."

"What does he mean, look in the trunk?" Grace said.

"I'll let you know, "I said, "after I look in the trunk."

I kept the motor running, set the emergency brake, popped the trunk, and got out. I wasn't eager to see what was waiting for me there, but I took a deep breath and lifted the lid. It wasn't my worst nightmare, but close. There it was, a labelled, digital copy of my performance on that TV show, Super Dupers, where I was humiliated in front of the viewing public for all to see. Attached to the case was a note. "You play it our way, and we bury this. We bought the rights. Otherwise, we'll use Project Bluebeam to project this video into the sky for all to see, and you'll be re-living it every month for the rest of your life. And don't think we can't do it, either." Signed, SG.

I closed the trunk and got back into my Bentley.

"Well, what was in there," Grace said. "Not a body, I hope."

"Just an idle threat and bad programming. Nothing to concern yourself with."

"While you were looking in the trunk, I couldn't help but wonder if you just proposed to me. Or would we only find that out in the future? I'm confused."

"We will see what we will see...I guess."

I winked at Grace and continued up the Lanes' driveway. Grace turned away from my wink, and staring straight ahead missed me with her delayed wink. Was she winking in wonderment at her possible future, or was she winking at no one?

"Why did they kidnap me, Joe?" she said, as we stopped in front of her girlhood mansion.

"I think it was to get my attention," I said.

"Are you saying I don't matter? I'm just along for the ride?"

She had a point. Was it all about me? It was a question I didn't want answered right now. Maybe later, when the bad guys had been defeated. Meanwhile, I hoped her mother was in a good mood.

CHAPTER FIFTEEN

Monday came fast and not so sweet. Alfred and Abner were in one of their moods, and I wasn't in the mood for theirs. I sat at my desk, reflecting. Doubts had been sown. Could Grace possibly be one of them? Sure, she'd come on strong at the beginning. Clever, insightful, witty, but the last few days she had come across as a little dimwitted. Was it all an act? And there was another problem eating away at me. My hardboiled detective thoughts were being undermined. I was beginning to lose my way of thinking, the way a good gumshoe should think, in hard, unemotional pulp fiction lingo. Although down deep I knew I had to let it all go. I was maturing. And for Grace's sake I needed to stay firmly planted in this century. She deserved as much, even if it did turn out that she was dimwitted. And then there was my writing course. I knew it had begun to change the way I thought, and I knew I had to wave goodbye to the old me, the illiterate detective, who thrived on ignorance. I was now awakening to reality, and sure I might backslide into the old ways once in a while, the way hardboiled detectives needed to think, but at heart that wasn't the real me anymore. The change had been made, and I had to agree with myself.

"How was yer lunch at the Lanes' yesterday?"

Abner said. "Was her mother kind to you, her future son-in-law?"

It was obvious Abner had decided to be irritating.

"Yes, lunch was enjoyable, thank you," I said.

"Ya know what they say," Abner said.

"No, Abner, what do they say?"

"You've seen the mother, so there's your future, as nice as ya think Grace is now."

"Insightful," Alfred said.

I had to admit there were going to be challenges. Mother was one of those quasi-intelligent, cultured people for which there was no hope. And to add uncertainty to our future family encounters she was stiffly religious. She'd been brought up in a religious home, she'd grown up religious, she'd looked at life in a religious way, she'd measured up, she'd treated others religiously. She'd married well. She'd dried on the vine. But there was hope for Grace. She wasn't like mother at all. Then, for some reason, I remembered I wanted to do a review of last week's writing lesson. It was a teaching on parallel structure.

But for now I needed to change the subject.

"Say, Abner, I'm wondering if you know anything about something called a Chronovisor."

"Ya, it's a load of hooey. They say they can look into the past. It's connected to fake time travel and time machines. The Vatican is supposed to have one stored somewhere."

"Do you think they can see into the future?" I said.

"The future? They can't even see into the past. The devil must be laughin' himself silly connin' them into thinkin' they are seein' the past. The demons are just makin' it up as they go along, like showin' them home movies."

"You'd make a great research assistant," Alfred said, "if your research was actually good for anything."

"And how about some project called Bluebeam?" I said. "Is there such a thing?"

"Sure there is. They're plannin' to put holographic projections in the sky to pretend there's an alien invasion. But it'll all be fake. NASA and the elite are behind it. They came up with it years ago, and now they've perfected it. The aliens are supposed to be coming to save us, but it's all demon stuff to bring in the New World Religion and the New World Order. We'll all be worshippin' Satan, if they pull it off."

So the bad guys and gals did have the technology to project my TV embarrassment into the clouds for all to see, that is, if I continued to work with the good guys and gals. Well, I was already committed, and if the good guys and gals didn't win, we were all lost, anyway. The whole world would be lost and the bad guys, and gals, would have won. And I would be dead anyway. And dead men don't blush.

"Have you come up with anything new on the kidnapping?" I said.

"Listen to him," Albner said. "He's pretendin' he cares."

"We don't know exactly why they would have

staged it," Alfred said.

"Ya, that we know," Abner said.

"But we are guessing they did it just to get the ball rolling," Alfred said.

"Ya, and you're the ball," Abner added.

I wanted to tell them about the Spelunkers' latest threat but knew if I did they'd have too many questions for me to answer.

I stood and walked over to the window. The snow had begun to fall again. Some nights now the air would sting your nostrils, not real bad, but bad enough to give you the hope that snow might soon fill your life, as the temperature dipped and the hope for a white Christmas excited the hearts of those like me up here in my penthouse office, and of those like them, down there, fighting it out in their dog-eat-dog lives. Snow was the great equalizer. But we didn't want a lot of snow. We Pacific Northwest people didn't want a lot of the white stuff. You know the kind of snow I mean, the kind we didn't want, the kind that comes in a heap in the night and then the temperature rises in the morning and then the slush begins, turning the white excitement of life into desperate grey, and then into the gritty blackness of utter despair. No, what we wanted was just enough snow to dust the place and ignite in our big-city hearts memories of Christmases past. Although when you thought back real hard you remembered the snow never fell perfect then either. Perfect snow was only a cheap trick your wistful memory played. Perfection, real perfection, was hard to come by in this life. Weather and memories were lousy candidates for perfection.

"What ya lookin' at?" Abner said. "Have ya never seen snow before? Just you wait. We'll be seein' a lot more of the white stuff. And I'm not talkin' about HAARP controllin' the weather, either."

"What now?" Alfred said.

"Yes, what now?" I said.

"We're headin' into a Grand Solar Minimum," Abner said. "Nobody's talkin' about it. But Global warmin's history. All those electric cars'll be chucked into the junk heap. One of the last times it happened was in the 1600s. Created a mini ice age. The sunspots stop happenin' and presto we're all livin' in igloos."

"Let's get back to the Spelunkers," Alfred said.

"You've had your warnin'," Abner said, concluding his climate forecast.

"Thank you, we'll keep it mind," Alfred said. "Now let's get on with it."

"Get on with what?" Abner said. "This is all pretend. He just wants to keep us busy so he can go on his secret mission with his girlfriend, the future Mrs. LaFlam."

I liked the sound of that. Mrs. Grace LaFlam. But what if she wanted to keep her maiden name? Then she would be Grace Lane LaFlam. Or whatever.

"Have you checked out the warehouse where they took Grace?" I said.

"Okay, let's go ahead and do that," Alfred said. "What do you think, Abner?"

"Sure, it beats sittin' around here waitin' for Christmas to come. And by the way, Mr. Casanova, are we havin' a staff Christmas party or not?"

"There's only three of us, plus Pen," I said. "What kind of party would that be?"

"Maybe you could spring for a dinner at a fancy restaurant then. You could bring your girlfriend, and maybe your Aunt Margaret might want to come."

"I'll think about it."

"Isn't that special? Our fearless leader is goin' to think about it."

"Let's go," Alfred said. "We'll grab some lunch on the way."

On their way out the door, Abner added, "If it's not too much of a burden, you might also give some thought to Christmas bonuses."

I was happy they were gone. I had some serious business to consider. What kind of Christmas present could you give a woman who had everything? And was it proper etiquette to roll two occasions into one, like for instance giving Grace an engagement ring at Christmas? That way I could kill two birds with one big stone. And as a nod to the day I could throw in a few stocking stuffers. Yes, it was a plan. But what about that other plan, the White Hat plan? What if Q and the Alliance decided it was time to begin the show before Christmas? I had to tell my inner child that such an outcome would be a blessing in disguise. I would then be justified in skipping gift-giving altogether, not to mention staff parties and bonuses.

I buzzed Pen.

"Hold my calls, I'm going for lunch."

"Couldn't you just tell me that on your way

out?" Pen said. "And why would I put someone's call through to an empty office, anyway?"

There was no point in arguing with her.

"You're right, as always," I said.

"I'm also going for lunch," she said. "And you might want to consider Abner's request in your spare time. But I won't hold my breath. I expect that you'll just carry on as usual with your selfish Scrooge mentality."

Pen had been listening in again, but I wasn't going to confront her.

"And I haven't been listening in, either, if that's what you think. Abner and I have already talked about it a few times before."

There was no sense asking her, "before what?" So I let it drop. She buzzed me off, and I was left to consider my future. Not my immediate future. That future was set. I was meeting Grace for lunch, and probably for dinner. Tonight's writing course was taking a break for the holidays. The second semester would begin in January. I was looking forward to it...unless.... I rose from my chair once more and surveyed the scene. Two armchairs and a sofa, my black leather seating ensemble languished there before my eyes, bereft of occupants. Would they ever be filled again? Would they ever be filled again in my presence, or would they remain, an impermanent testimony to my impermanent life? Joe LaFlam, the detective who cared, was whisked from the planet to his promised eternal dwelling place, his soul carrying wistful memories of earth, the cobwebs left to embrace his now forgotten dream. And what then of Abner and Alfred? Would they then turn one last time to gaze at their mentor's unhappy desk, choking back tears, and without a word depart and be gone?

I snapped out of it. Grace was waiting.

CHAPTER SIXTEEN

I asked Grace if she would bless our lunch.

"Would you say Grace?" I said.

"Why would I say Grace? I don't want to talk to myself."

"I mean, would you bless the food," I said.

"Oh, I see, how silly of me."

There she was again, sowing doubts in my mind. Was she simply simple-minded, or was she leading me on for reasons yet unknown? And why was she so agreeable to take part in the Alliance's plan? Was she just putting a brave face forward, or was she unable to grasp the consequences of her willing participation. And her role was not a minor one; she was in a starring role. Not a role superior to mine, of course, but complementary to mine, a role that would help to highlight my heroic stand. Or, on the other hand, was she one of them, a daughter of the elite, an accomplice in her own kidnapping, whose purpose was to draw me into their wicked scheme and entice me with her female wiles, wiles she possessed in overflowing quantities.

She blessed our meal and then said, "I think if we remain calm and develop our relationship, as we are waiting for the Alliance to set their plan in motion, then we will be functioning well enough as a couple, and as partners in this endeavor of all endeavors, to be in an adequate state of preparedness to be able to meet any contingency the devil's pawns might assail us with."

"You've got that right," I said, and slurped a spoonful of my split pea soup.

How could she, from one minute to the next, shift from simplemindedness to a brilliant summation of our circumstances? No there was more here than met the eye, and there was plenty to meet the eye, but I couldn't stay fixated on that aspect of her being. I wasn't the first hapless victim to slide down that slippery slope to oblivion, my lustful self having ignored wisdom's plea. Yes, there was more to this relationship than met the eye, and I aimed to find out the truth.

"The show must go on," she said, for no apparent reason, and then took a preliminary nibble of her cucumber sandwich.

So there it was. I needed to play my cards close to the chest. There was no sense in knocking myself out by giving her the third degree. There was no reason to go rough on her, but sooner or later I would know the score. She turned away to survey the joint, and I gave her the once over again. She was easy on the eyes alright and I wasn't going to upset the applecart, the way a detective could stir the pot, if he set his mind to it. No, I would bide my time. I was a detective, the way a guy could be a detective, when the dice were rolled and the clues fell like dominoes in a game of chance. I stopped. My hardboiled thoughts had taken over again. Abner was right. My writing course had confused my identity. Was my personality fragmenting, or was I simply growing? I hoped I would become the real me in the end. The real Joe. And didn't we all want to be the real "us"? But of course we wouldn't be the final real "us" until we passed from this world into eternity. In the meantime, we needed to make the most of our time here, and I aimed to.

"Where are you, Joe?" she said.

"I'm right here," I said. "The same old Joe. I know who I am and the mission set before me. My identity is solid. I have a firm foundation, and I live without any fear of personality fragmentation."

"No, I mean, in our relationship. Do you love me, Joe?"

She was getting down to brass tacks now. My answer might possibly seal my future, but if she turned out to be one of them, then what?

"You know I do," I said.

"That's all I needed to know," she said.

I was glad that was over with. Love was a hard one. It could commit you for life. And I needed to know who Grace was before I spilled my heart. I'd been played for a sucker before, and it hadn't been pretty, the way love could be ugly when the loved object was a crooked dame, taking you for all the pain she could dish out.... I stopped in time before hardboiled Joe made more of his thoughts known. My identity was floating around in a sea of consciousness, searching for a place to call home. Who was I? And who was I becoming? For one thing, I was becoming concerned, but not concerned enough to seek professional counseling. Sure, I had myself well under control.

"How about you?" I said.

"Don't be silly, Joe, of course I do."

That settled, we finished our lunch.

CHAPTER SEVENTEEN

Back at the office, I waited for my partners to return. It was late afternoon. I hadn't decided about a staff party yet. How could I? What if I was called away to save the planet? Who would make the arrangements then? No, I had to stall. There was no telling what might happen next.

My intercom buzzed. It was Pen. She had returned from her four hour lunch.

"Well?" she said.

"I haven't decided yet."

"You mean about a staff party or about bonuses?"

"Neither one."

She buzzed me off.

My partners breezed through the door. Abner was humming Jingle Bells. Alfred sat down in one of the armchairs and Abner flopped on the couch.

"Any leads from the warehouse?" I said.

"No," Alfred said.

"You didn't expect we'd find anythin', did ya?" Abner said.

"What if she wasn't even at that warehouse, and she made the whole thing up?" Alfred said.

I didn't like the way Alfred was casting aspersions on my dear Grace, but since I had already cast the same aspersions it would have been hypocritical of me to call him on it.

"Are you calling her a liar, and worse?" I said.

"He's just sayin'," Abner said, defending Alfred for a change. "Besides, we both think yer bein' taken for a ride again."

"It's my ride," I said.

"Yer deluded," Abner said.

"What do you know about delusion?" I said.

"Plenty, ya don't live the life of an alcoholic fer most of yer life and think ya got it together."

"No, I mean, what do you know about delusion? How do you know what you believe is true? I mean how do you even know if this physical world is real? And how do you know if your identity is solid?"

"So we're getting philosophical now, are we?" Alfred said. "It's a little late for that. You've got her all lined up for a trip down the aisle, and now you sound like you're not so sure."

"Don't worry about bein' deluded," Abner said. "The whole world's bein' deluded. It's mass psychosis. People believe what the news tells 'em. We're bein' programmed by popular music and TV and it's all lies. We're in the Matrix, and unless ya swallow the red pill yer doomed to livin' yer life as a slave to the elites. They're workin' on it overtime. One ring to rule 'em all, and the devil's forgin' the ring now. We're headin' fer the Great Tribulation and most of the folk in the world don't even know it. And they're sure not goin' to be able to escape to no parallel earth in the Multiverse, before anythin' bad happens. Cause there ain't no such thing. The Book says ya die once and after that the Judgment."

"Thank you for that bit of enlightenment," Alfred said. "And no, we're not curious enough to learn anything more about parallel earths, thank you."

So, if Abner was right, I had been programmed my whole life to believe the lie. And was my hardboiled self just an attempt to escape reality, to go back to a more safe and predictable time, to bring order out of personal chaos, to confront the cruel callous world on its own terms? Time would tell.

"Should we tell him now," Alfred said.

"Sure, why not, he needs a wake-up call," Abner said.

"Tell me what?" I said.

"You tell him, Abner," Alfred said.

"There ain't no warehouse at the corner of Victoria Street and Marine Drive."

The news hit my gut like a blow from a wrecking ball. But I wasn't going to let them see me fold, like a poker star tossing in his 4 and 7 off-suit hole cards.

I groaned, exhaled, and said, "Do you think the police know?"

"They most likely didn't follow up after she was returned safely," Alfred said.

"Did you check the cab company's log?" I said.

"Are you kiddin'," Abner said. "You mean we shoulda checked for a fare from an address that don't exist?"

So, the game was on. The subterfuge was exposed. Grace was...who? But maybe she was simply misguided. No, that didn't work. Or maybe she was just a spoiled rich kid playing a game. No, that made no sense. I didn't want to think about that other possibility, the one I had already considered, and the one Alfred had already so rudely spoken. What if...? I had to confront Grace, or maybe I didn't. It was hard to know, but I would know when the time came. Why pluck up a budding relationship when love was in the air?

CHAPTER EIGHTEEN

The next day came hard and fast. Grace and I had a tense dinner the night before. Grace's cod was watery, and the batter on my entree was mushy near the halibut's flesh. All in all, fish and chips were a bad choice for a romantic tête-à-tête. Not that our têtes were in harmony anyway, given the deceit lingering in the air. We ended our evening at her parents' door. I managed to issue a peck on her cheek. That was the best I could do. I hoped she didn't think the less of me for my effort, or suspect that I knew of her lying ways.

I had been awakened by Leo at 6:00 a.m. The game was on, he said. There went Christmas. Oh, well. He told me to meet him in a familiar spot, the park on Little Mountain. I pulled in at 7:15 and waited. He was taking his time. I'd just begun playing Free Cell on my phone when Leo's Mercedes pulled up beside me. He had friends with him, two of them. All three of them got out of their car, and then the guy who was supposed to be Leo knocked on my driver's window. But he wasn't Leo, and neither of the two henchmen was Leo's driver Snub Nose. I had a problem. The guy who wasn't Leo pointed his 9mm at me and waved for me to open my door. I complied.

"You're coming with us," he said.

"You're not Leo," I said.

"Who's Leo?" he said.

I was beginning to get a bad feeling about this. If the Alliance hadn't sent them, then this could mean only one thing. Spelunkers. I got out of the car.

"Did the head of the Spelunkers send you?" I said.

"Don't crack wise with me," the guy said, who wasn't Leo.

"I wasn't cracking wise," I said. "And why are you talking like that? I'm the hardboiled detective, not you."

"Shut up and get in the car," he said.

Goon-one drove and goon-two rode shotgun. The guy who wasn't Leo got in the back with me.

"Do you mind if I call you Leo?" I said.

"They told me you were a wise guy, but I'm not going to put up with it."

He produced a small canister from his coat pocket and sprayed a short burst at my face. As my lights were going out, a cameo of Grace appeared in my mind and then faded away. I wondered if I would ever marry.

I came-to lying on a bottom bunk. The room was dark, except for a bunny night-light plugged into a wall socket. My head felt like a party piñata that had been smashed by a Louisville Slugger, sending my not so prized thoughts exploding into my fractured reality hither and yon. In the chaos I heard a faint whimper. The top bunk was occupied. The blood rushed to my concussion, as I stood to see who my bunkmate might be. I peered over the edge. She opened her eyes and stared back at me.

"Oh, Joe," Grace said. "I didn't think I would ever see you again."

"Nor I, you," I said. "You were the last thing I thought of as I lost consciousness."

"I love being kidnapped with you. I feel so safe when you're with me."

"Are you okay?" I said.

"Oh, silly, I'm fine, but I could use a Matcha Latté."

"I'll ring for room service."

"Funny, Joe. You're so clever."

I helped her down. And even though she had gone through an ordeal, she still smelled good, and I got lost there, in the aroma of Grace, and in the sensuality of an almost hug, my headache fleeing. But then upon momentary reflection, I wondered if my headache was just beginning? But no, I wasn't going to bring up the annoying fact that she wasn't kidnapped the first time, and what was that all about? No, I was going to bide my time and see who our kidnappers were and discover what they wanted from us. We didn't have long to wait.

Goon-Two opened the door, and ushered us out of the room. He led us down a long dark, carpeted hall, with rooms on either side, not unlike the second floor of a Ramada Inn. But my detective sense told me we were deep underground. Goon-Two stopped at the end of the hall and opened a door to our right. He motioned for us to go in. The sprayer who wasn't Leo was waiting for us.

"Hi, Leo," I said. "Thanks for the nap."

"Don't call me Leo," he said. "You can call me Victor."

"Is Vic your name?" I said.

"Yes," Vic said. "Still the smart guy, are we?"

Vic led us into the room. It was poorly lit and decorated in an early cave motif, complete with primitive wall drawings. In one corner of the room a glittering lava lamp slinked its mesmerizing essence.

"Here they are," Vic said to the head resting on the back of a bean bag chair.

The head turned and spoke, as its body rose to greet us, crunching the beans.

"Welcome to one floor above upper-hell," the head said. It was attached to a tall thin body, wearing a black lounge suit.

"It's him," Grace said. "It's the kidnapper's voice. He must be the kidnapper."

I nodded at Grace's insight.

"And can you smell it?" she said. "It's that same vanilla smell."

"Neatly noticed," the head said. "It's my vanilla scented cologne."

"So, are you the one in charge around here?" I said.

"No, I'm only your guide. They call me Deep Blue. You will meet the head of our movement in due time."

"May I call you DB?" I said.

"Yes, if you wish, but you needn't try to provoke me. It won't work, so you would be wise not to try."

"Thanks for the advice. So where are you supposed to be guiding us?"

"It's not so much where, as it is through. My task is to guide you through your indoctrination."

"And suppose I don't want to be indoctrinated?"

"Oh, but you will. And I do hope you can appreciate that we have preempted your stupid Q mission of infiltrating our movement. The Alliance has inaccurately characterized us as the wicked Spelunkers, evil to the core. And your amateurish mission was intended to expose us for the whole world to see. All very heroic, I'm sure. But we were way ahead of them, and the ridiculous plan would never have worked. Our quantum computer is miles ahead of theirs. That's how we knew where to meet you and how we were able to get there before they did. Ours is smarter. Besides, we have a much better future planned for you both than they ever had. They probably weren't even going to pay you, were they, or maybe only a pittance? You were supposed to undertake their mission out of the goodness of your heart and then be satisfied to revel in the warm fuzzies of having saved humanity from the devil. We couldn't take the chance that you would go forward with their plan, even though we warned you against it. So we decided to prevent you from making that fatal mistake."

So there it was, just as I suspected. We were pawns in a quantum computer game, a game that would decide the fate of the world. And in the end whose side were we going to be on? Better still, whose side was Grace on?

"You mean, we're going to work for the devil?" I said.

"Precisely, but it's not as bad as you might think. In fact, he has chosen you for an exalted position, the position of the anti-Christ. You'll be on the top of the heap, bucko, as long as you know what's good for you. And, of course, we decided to bring your bride along, since you are so smitten with her. She will be the anti-Christ's Mrs., or your partner as they like to say these days."

"I'm in the room," Grace said.

"So you are, my dear, and I'm assuming wherever Joe goes you will go, and whatever Joe faces, you will face, for good or ill, in happiness or sadness, come riches or poverty...."

"Cut the lyricism," I said. "I learned all about that literary device in Lesson #10 of my writing course, and I'm not impressed."

"I think it's a sweet sentiment," Grace said. "And don't you worry, Joe. I'm definitely committed to going with you."

Grace winked at me. I wasn't in the winking mood.

"Don't be mad, Joe," she said. "Being in charge of the world won't be that bad."

Grace was tempting me. And I knew at that moment how Adam must have felt. And why he made that unwitting choice to take humanity down the long winding road of corruption, pain, and death. He must have known then he was only a pawn in the game, a game that would take millennia to complete. He must have taken a long, hard gulp when he realized he'd lost the farm, and because of him and his bad decision, humanity would buy the farm generation after generation until the end of time. And here I stood at the end of the game, at the end of time as we knew it. Well, I wasn't going to make the same eternal mistake as he did. But in the meantime, I would play along with the evil crew for as long as it took to bring the Spelunkers to their knees and defeat Old Slewfoot in the bargain.

"So when do we meet the big boss?" I said.

"At just the exact perfect moment," Deep Blue said.

"Ooh, how exciting," Grace said.

CHAPTER NINETEEN

Deep Blue himself led us back to our room and left us there. I heard the key turn in the lock. We were prisoners. That's when temptation struck me hard. Here we were the two of us, bunkmates, locked in with each other and locked into the devil's scheme. I couldn't see any place in the room where cameras might be hidden. We were alone. I sat on the side of the lower bunk and Grace joined me. We had only the bunny light for company. Had I been a non-believer I would have likely had impure thoughts. Although, being a believer I also had impure thoughts. But my distrust saved me from making the mistake of a lifetime, since I didn't know who Grace was. Sure, taken at face value, she was all a man might ever want in a wife. But going deeper might reveal an ugly detail. She might be a willing pawn of the devil.

"So, what should we do now?" Grace said.

"Bide our time," I said.

"How do we do that?" she said.

"If they had left us our phones, we could have played FreeCell," I said.

"Ironic," she said.

"Why's that?"

"Don't you see? We're not free in this cell and we can't play FreeCell either."

"Clever insight," I said.

There she was. At it again. One minute witless, the next, pointing out ironies. I knew from my PI training that inconsistency was a method of control. If you kept people off balance, so that they didn't know what to expect next, you could manipulate them to do your will. Well, I wasn't going to fall for it. And I wasn't going to pop the question, either. I wasn't going to ask why she faked her kidnapping. But since there wasn't anything better to do.

"There's something I've been meaning to ask you," I said.

"Oh, Joe, ask me anything. I'm here for you. I'll answer any question that is in my power to answer, and I also would help you in any other way I am able."

"Well, if you're sure you want to, then why did you fake your kidnapping? There's no warehouse at the corner of Victoria Street and Marine Drive."

"Oh, Joe! Why do you doubt me? It was dark and I was blindfolded. Yes, I might have been mistaken about where I was taken. I got all mixed up. It was a traumatic experience, and even you bringing it up again makes me feel all fearful inside."

"What about the cab ride" I said. I wasn't going to let her off the hook that easy. "You said you had your phone and you called a cab. Where did you tell them to pick you up?"

"I phoned from outside the building. As soon as the kidnappers left I wanted to get out of there as fast as I could. I panicked and went out onto the street and walked, I don't know how far, and then I called a taxi.

I must have just told them the street I was on at the time. But who cares, Joe. What difference at this point does it make? All that matters is us, and our mission, and God, and the devil, and our future together."

"Good enough," I said.

Who was I to doubt her? I was only a pawn in their game. But was she a pawn in their game, too? Or was she one of their minions? Those were the questions that needed to be answered. Another question that needed to be answered was about my identity. I had been identifying as a hardboiled detective for years, but now that identity was slipping away. I could hardly think hardboiled anymore. My new identity had been birthed in my writing class. But how might a literate detective flourish? And could I now identify as literate? A Joe LaFlam, Literate Detective Agency might not sell too well in the PI market. These were challenges that would need to be faced. And how would Alfred and Abner fit into our new literate agency? Certainly Abner wouldn't, but Alfred probably would.

"Are you there?" Grace said. "You certainly like to daydream, don't you? What do you think about when you're lost in one of your trances?"

I decided she needed a straight answer.

"Just now I was thinking about identity," I said."

"Identity? What do you mean? You're you, Joe, and nobody can be a better you than you are, Joe. So don't worry, my darling Joe."

So now I was her darling. I had to think fast,

or I would fall under her spell. She continued to smell good and looked even better.

"How do you identify?" I said.

"Identify? Oh, that's just silly, Joe. I'm a woman and you're a man, what else do we need to know?"

"Good summary," I said.

She moved closer. Her eyes grasped mine with hers. I was sunk, but then Providence arrived in the form of Deep Blue. He'd opened the door when I was lost in the essence of Grace, in that moment when I didn't care who she was at her core.

"Okay, you lovebirds," Deep Blue said. "It's time to get acquainted with your future."

"How do you identify?" I said. "They must call you Deep Blue for a reason."

"I'm gender fluid. And, I must say, it's so kind of you to ask. I'm as free as the deep blue sea, and my pronoun is they."

"How about you?" they said.

"I've been having challenges lately. I'm afraid that my hardboiled identity is fading away. And my literate identity hasn't yet settled in, if in fact that's the kind of detective I'm meant to be."

"Don't you worry, my boy, the anti-Christ identity will sort you out fast."

"You have the potential to be anything you want to be, Joe," Grace said. "Anti-Christ or no anti-Christ."

I appreciated her encouragement.

"All right," they said. "Come with me. I'll take you to the screening room where you will gain a better understanding of our mission and your place in it. And yes, my dear, I know it's your mission too. And I do know you're in the room."

"How sweet," Grace said. "Maybe you gender fluid people do have some redeeming qualities. Sensitivity to others is extremely important."

"Come along then," they said.

Deep Blue led us back down that same hall, and then we went through a door leading to a large theater with a seating capacity of about five hundred. We took our seats, but instead of focusing on the stage in front of us, our seats flipped back and we were left staring at a 50-foot square screen that had descended from the ceiling and had stopped about 30-feet above us.

"Ooh, how avant-garde," Grace said.

"What's showing?" I said to them/they.

"You'll see. It's all about you, Joe. Yes, and you too, Grace."

The credits began to roll. It was a Second Heaven production, directed by someone called The Fabricator. The executive producer was none other than Satan himself. The show began with a baby in the womb and then the baby grew to become a male child of about five years old playing with a stick and then he became an awkward teenager wearing pants that are too short and then he became an awkward adult looking up at the sky in search of meaning. And, of course, it was all me. Not an actor playing the part of me, but it was actually me. I'd been watched my whole life it seemed. But why, and by whom? Then the words Identity and Destiny crawled across the screen in large black caps. That got my attention. Was I now going to find the answer? Was I finally going to learn who I was and what I was destined to become? Or at least discover the devil's version of me.

Then a history lesson of me and my lineage appeared in the form of a family tree that went back as far as the Garden of Eden. And as providence would have it, I was a descendent of Cain, or at least that's who the narrator said I was. He sounded a lot like Deep Blue. The show culminated with the assertion that I was the seed of the Serpent and therefore immensely qualified to be the anti-Christ for my generation, a generation that would wind up all things and deliver the world into the hands of the Devil, himself, the rightful ruler of planet earth. But it seemed to me like I'd seen this movie before. And I wasn't convinced. The credits began to roll and our seats flipped upright.

"Oh, Joe," Grace said. "I had no idea you were so important."

I needed to play along for the sake of humanity. This was my ticket in, and once in, under my benevolent rule, I would be able to dismantle and destroy the Spelunkers and all they stood for. And next in my sights would be the devil. But this plan was the same one the Alliance's quantum computer had also conceived. Although the Alliance had skipped the part about me being the Serpent's spawn. And then I wondered if the Spelunkers' and the Alliance's computers had been talking to each other behind their humans' backs. No matter, I was in for the ride of my life, and I had my bride riding the roller coaster along with me, that is, if she really was my bride, and not someone else's coaster mate. If she did belong to another, there was a good chance I would finish the treacherous ride on my knees in a pool of shame, embarrassed and throwing up my hot dogs and candy floss.

But right now I needed to put up some resistance. I didn't want to seem too easy.

"That can't be true," I said. "I'm a Christian now."

"Are you sure?" they said. "Haven't you always felt a little out of place in the church?"

"Doesn't everybody?" I said.

"No, you're not getting it. The reason you don't feel connected to them is because you're not one of them. You belong to us, and with us."

"Hmm...now that you mention it," Grace said, "I've never felt like I belonged in church either."

"You see, Joe," they said, "she's the perfect mate for you. Both of you are ours. The Boss will be so pleased that you two love-birds have come to your senses without the need to convince you further."

So according to the Spelunkers I was predestined to be one of them. I made a mental note that if I ever did meet up with John Calvin in the hereafter, I would have a few words with him. Nit-picking aside, I needed to get on with the business at hand.

"We'll be together no matter what," Grace said.

I was really beginning to wonder if Grace was living in an altered reality. And what could she possibly see in me, other than, of course, my having a future as the anti-Christ?

But that was wrong thinking. I needed to stop the self-criticism and the questioning of my identity. For one thing, I was a detective, and a darn good one at that. Sure, there would always be those who would try to make me feel like less of a man, including myself at times, and those who would try to make me feel like dirt, including myself at times. And why? Because I'd chosen to scour the underbelly of society for meaning to my existence. Draining the swamp was a job that needed to be done, so why shouldn't a Christian detective be the one to do it? And now the ultimate job lay before me, the ultimate case that would etch me in the annals of history as one of the greats, not just one of the greatest Christian detectives, and definitely not one of the greatest anti-Christs, but one of the greatest detectives of any kind, and maybe, just maybe, as the greatest detective of all time. What an identity! All I had to do was stay the course, pretend I've fallen to the depths of depravity, and then confront the devil before he corrupted the whole human race. And then again I knew that only God could put the cuffs on the devil.

"Where did you go, Joe?" Grace said. "Were you daydreaming about us again, and seeing us united as one?"

She was attempting to create my thoughts for me. A bad sign.

"I know where Joe went," they said. "He was contemplating his great future running the world with his darling Grace by his side."

"I'm in the room," Grace said.

CHAPTER TWENTY

They had taken us back to our cell, where they told us to wait for an invitation to attend an audience with the head cheese. Not Lucifer himself, but his First Minister. Polly he was called, short for Apollyon I found out later, and he had been known to call that Old Serpent his pal Lucy. Pretty cosy relationship. By all accounts they were an informal, friendly bunch of eternally damned beings. Grace and I had been given back our phones. She was trying to sign on without the password, while I was content to play FreeCell, ironic or not.

"Do you know what Abner told me?" I said.

"No. How could I know what he told you unless you gave me a hint?"

"You're not supposed to know," I said. "That's just an introduction to what I want to tell you."

"Oh, I see. What did Abner tell you?"

"It's about our phones. He told me the CIA and DARPA started Facebook, and that Zuckerberg is just the front man."

"Weird. What's DARPA?"

"I don't know what it stands for, but according to Abner, it's some kind of military technology research project."

"Just more conspiracy theories," Grace said. "As

far as I've heard, there's no end to them. Abner's okay, but he wouldn't be the type of person I'd choose to help me navigate through life's challenges."

"Insightful," I said.

"Have you decided what you're going to do?" Grace said. "I don't know how you are going to reconcile being a believer in Christ and at the same time be the anti-Christ. I know the Alliance's plan was for you to pretend to be the anti-Christ, but who are we going to believe now? If it's true that you're the Seed of the Serpent and there's no way you can get out of it, then what? The Alliance didn't tell us anything about that. You were only supposed to pretend to be one of them. And you were only supposed to pretend you were a prime candidate for the position of ant-Christ by showing them what was supposed to be your fake lineage. So now what? You are a descendent of Cain or you're not. You're a devil worshiper or you're not. Although I must say your film biography looked extremely convincing to me."

There she was again, suddenly wearing her thinking cap. But the question remained. Was AI playing us all for suckers?

"Thanks for the summary," I said. "But either way there's no going back. You can leave if you want to. In fact, I urge you to go back to your life of privilege above ground, where the subterranean cares of this world rarely poke up their ugly heads for all to see. Go back before it's too late."

"Oh, Joe, you're so caring. But I don't want to be anywhere where you are not. Our lives are inextricably intertwined now. There's no place for me up there among the wealthy, knowing that what happens down here will inevitably invade our happy, naïve lives of privilege and contentment. And I also want to end up on the winning side. That is why I have cast my lot with you, Joe. You are a winner, no matter what your choice might be in the end."

So, her decision to come with me was based more on logic than romance. And on winning. I hadn't been looking for a platonic relationship, but you got what you got in this life, and it was what it was, no matter what. But there was too much going on right now for me to go about the task of deconstructing our relationship. Besides, if her heart was true and the knot was tied certain connubial privileges were implied.

"Thanks for your support," I said. "I hope to be all that you hope me to be."

"I know you will be, Joe. Yes, I know you will be."

"In the end, when all is said and done, I only want to do what God wants me to do."

"God's not like us, Joe. He's far above us and our little trials."

The fate of the world didn't seem to me like a little trial, but it was obvious that Grace had her own way of looking at things.

"I'm counting on that," I said.

CHAPTER TWENTY-ONE

We continued our vigil in our secluded cell, waiting for the call from Polly. I was pensive, and Grace seemed content to play with her phone and watch me think.

"What's a Metaverse?" she said, holding up her phone, as if her question was hidden in there somewhere. "I heard it's the new thing."

"I don't know, but Abner says it's some kind of Internet place where you live your life in a made up world. They've got glasses now that you wear to join other people in on-line communities and you do things."

"Fascinating. Do you think it will catch on?"

"It's one way to escape from the trials of this world, I guess."

"This world isn't that bad, is it, Joe?"

She had to be kidding.

"Abner says it's just one more way the devil is going to use to get people distracted, so he can take over."

"Are you going to stop him, Joe? Or are you going to join him. Have you decided yet?"

"Only God can stop him. We're only the players on the stage, destined to act our part in the unfolding of the story."

"How poetic, Joe. You should have been a writer."

I wasn't insulted, only discouraged. To change the subject, I said, "Then there's the Multiverse."

"I've heard of that, too, Joe. What is it?"

"It's hard to understand."

"Oh, I see."

"There are lots of them, and they're supposed to be parallel to this one. And there are other versions of you and me living in them. I haven't looked into it myself. I only know what I hear from Abner. And he can be difficult to follow most of the time."

"What do we need them for, Joe, those other places? I mean, isn't this world good enough? We should be working on making this one better and not escaping into other realities on the Internet and into other universes, parallel or not, or being duplicates of us. Where is it all headed, Joe?"

"Not to worry. We only need to stay focused and do our part right now. And right now we need to hear from Polly and uncover what's next on their agenda."

"You're so wise, Joe. I only want to be in the world where you are, and you're right here. I don't need to play pretend on the Internet, or escape to parallel worlds. This world is good enough for me as long as I'm with you, my darling Joe."

If Grace was one of them, she was certainly overplaying her part in the devil's game. But if she was who she said she was, then she was certainly overplaying her part in the mating game. Either way I needed to be on my toes. Grace was elusive. There was no doubt about that.

"But did anyone ever know another person really? Sure, you could live together for 50 years and discover each other's pluses and minuses, but did you ever get to know the other person down deep, where the rubber met the road, where one's oft broken heart limped its way onward in its journey through life, longing for its eternal home?"

Grace seemed to be following my thoughts. She nodded knowingly and said, "You're thinking out loud, Joe. But it's so kind of you to let me into your mental world."

"Oh, I'm sorry," I said. "I didn't mean to alarm you."

"I hope they come back soon," she said.

I got the message. This wasn't an ensuite cell, and I wasn't the only one who needed to use the powder room. I guessed that Grace wanted to freshen up, even though she continued to smell good.

In the nick of time, the door opened and Deep Blue appeared. They asked if we needed anything before we met Apollyon, the First Minister. We expressed our immediate needs, and they obliged us by leading each of us to our respective rooms of choice. Once we had prepared for the audience, Deep Blue led us back down the hallway, where we stepped into an elevator. It lacked a floor numbering panel, but it seemed to me that we descended a few floors, and then we stopped. The doors opened to reveal what looked like a pit of hell. Seated amid the inferno, on what I assumed was a flame resistant throne, was a being who was a dead ringer for an aging Henry Kissinger. He was dressed in red tights, with a joker's crown sitting side-saddle on his head. In his left hand he held an ebony sceptre topped by a cobra's head.

"Turn down the flames, Bill," Polly thundered. "It's too hot in here for my new friends to endure."

So Deep Blue was, in fact, just plain Bill. Good to know. Polly gestured with his cobra sceptre for us to sit. Our chairs had been placed about ten feet in front of the throne. They were red, pulsing, brimstone rocks. We hesitated to sit down on the hot seats.

"Don't worry, already," Polly said. "They cooled off eons ago. We light them up now for effect. And by the way, welcome to upper-hell."

We sat and waited for our futures to unfold, for good, or for who knew?

"Okay, so here's the pitch," Polly said. "We're in need of an anti-Christ figure for the times we are living in, and you, my dear Joe, are just the ticket. Your genes are the perfect match."

"So what...?"

"Don't interrupt, Joe. I've got a lot to say and time is short, if you catch my meaning. Lucy...I mean Lucifer, the Big Boss down below, is anxious to get the show on the road."

Polly went on to explain my role in the last days push to establish Lucifer's reign on earth. As it turned out, I was simply the front man. Lucifer himself was going to give me supernatural power to subdue the nations. Grace offered me a few ambiguous winks during Polly's spirited presentation, but my wariness of Polly's pitch had left me winkless. Polly ended with a wink of his own, originating it seemed to me from the depths of depravity.

"Oh, Joe," Grace said. "I can't wait to start a family."

Most would have taken Grace's exclamation as surprisingly out of place, but I was beginning to know her better. No, she wasn't one of them, and she wasn't one of the White Hats, either. She didn't care. She was only dedicated to establishing our future together, no matter what in the world was going on. She was, indeed, a woman for all seasons, and for all times, and for all circumstances, and she was all mine. My prayers had been finally answered. There was only one small matter left. Polly now seemed open for question period.

"So how do the Spelunkers fit into the plan?" I said.

"Just a cover story, my boy. The Spelunkers, the Illuminati, the Cabal, the Deep State, the rich families, Big Tech, the media, all pawns in the game, along with the heads of apostate Christianity and the false religions. We are looking forward to welcoming the leaders here. They have all played their part, knowingly or unknowingly, but either way, it's no matter. Their descent will be magnificent. We will keep them occupied here for a very long time, as their reward for a job well done. And once you have accomplished your appointed task, Joe, you will be given the honour of being their overseer."

So, I was condemned to hell for eternity, too. The anti-Christ business was a tough one. Grace began to squirm in her chair.

She whispered in my ear, "Did I miss something, Joe? I don't get it. Is my family going to be imprisoned here, too?"

"Looks like," I whispered back. "And I don't think, the way things are going, that we'll have time to raise a family, either."

Grace hardened. I could feel her resolve, and it was nothing to mess with.

Polly continued on, "And we have a special place for those who promoted the fallacy that mankind would ascend to a higher dimension on the basis of thinking and believing higher thoughts. Raising their vibrations, what a joke! New Agers we called them. I coined the term myself. And we conned them into thinking they were on a journey to meet other ascended beings from other places in the universe. The Andromedans, for instance. What a hoot!"

So much for the Age of Aquarius, I thought. And there were some aging, hippy Baby Boomers whose worlds were going to be rocked, not to mention those current neo-hippies tripping on ignorance.

"All those wonderful deceivers have a special place prepared for them here, along with those who taught reincarnation. Lucy, I mean The Boss, had quite an evil chuckle over those suckers who swallowed that bunch of nonsense hook, line, and sinker. Imagine, believing you can go around again for another try if you didn't get it right the first thousand times."

I needed to ask Polly if Abner had his facts straight.

"Do you mind if I ask you a few more important questions now?

Polly issued an imperious nod, one hand righting his slipping crown, the other holding his cobra sceptre firmly.

"What about the Draco Reptilians?" I said.

"Oh, that one. We're the Reptilians. We have the Reptilian Brigade out in full force. Some of them are running countries and others are busy working to establish a one world government. But they will eventually be working for you, Joe, after the Great Reveal. And, of course, we have the UFO anti-gravity, aerial, acrobatic team, dipsy-doodling around in the atmosphere, giving folks a good show."

So, Abner was right again.

"While I've got you here, then what about the Multiverse and parallel universes?"

"Oh, that's an offshoot of our LSD and ayahuasca department. Our experts in the field lead people to believe while they're under the influence that there are many levels of reality. They call it spiritual experience, but it's really only the drugs short-circuiting their nervous systems."

"And the Multiverse and parallel worlds are related to that?"

"It's a simple extrapolation. We encouraged the world's scientists to get involved and then led them on a merry chase of discovery until they arrived at the conclusion that there are many universes, ones you can't see in this light spectrum. Of course, the reason you can't see them is because they don't exist in any spectrum. But we won't let them get far enough to discover that. We often exploit the fact that people will go to great lengths to avoid the obvious."

"And what's the obvious?" I wanted to know.

"We don't talk about that around here, Joe."

Grace stood and began to sidle toward the elevator.

"Don't leave Grace," Polly said. "We're not bad beings, and once you get to know us I'm sure you will see us in a whole new light. And besides, you can't leave here unless I give the word."

"Yes, come back, Grace," I said.

"I will, Joe, but only because you say so."

Grace returned to her brimstone. I was encouraged. I'd asked her to do something, and she had complied. Of course, I wasn't one of those dominant males who insisted their wives were to be totally subservient to the will of their husband and master. Still, I'd never had a woman do what I said before. And although I definitely wouldn't make a habit in the future of forcing my will on Grace, I had to admit I took some pleasure in her obedience.

"I don't want to take advantage of your hospitality," I said, "But I've got a partner who tells me about all these conspiracy theories. For instance, there's DARPA and HAARP...."

"Ahhh, of course, those government agencies

are just low level players in the game. The CIA and all that crew are useful in destabilizing various areas of the world and taking the drugs to market, and as far as HAARP goes, well, weather modification is old hat. No need to go into it any further. Suffice to say it serves its purpose."

I realized I had to apologize to Abner, that is, if I ever saw him again.

"So what's the next step?" I said. "When do I begin taking over the world?"

"Cool your heels, Joe," Polly said. "We're just getting started. You need to be instructed in how to perform miracles and do fake signs and wonders. And that's not easy. Extensive training sessions are required."

"What about me?" Grace said.

"You, my dear, will be an indispensible partner on Joe's road to anti-Christ maturity."

"But what does that mean?" she said.

"Wherever Joe goes you will go, and whatever Joe faces, you will face, for good or ill, in happiness or sadness, come riches or poverty...."

"Not that again," I said, and Grace agreed. "Is that some standard line you use on all your converts?"

"Perverting marriage is one of our most effective devices. It prevents people from living happy lives."

"Diabolical," I said.

"I don't care for it here," Grace said.

Grace was souring on our mission, and that gave me greater hope that she was genuine, and genuinely mine. Life couldn't get any better than this, except for the anti-Christ part.

CHAPTER TWENTY-TWO

Deep Blue took us back to our cell. I was deep in thought, processing our interview with Polly. I'd never in my life felt that I was a demon-seed condemned to hell. In fact, I'd always thought I was a pretty good guy, a little short on understanding maybe, and perhaps somewhat naïve in my early PI days, but never someone destined to serve the devil. No, their genealogy had to be a fake and intended to lead me into servitude. But why me? They had the ability to fake anyone's family tree. There had to be a reason they picked me. But I had another nagging question. How was I going to bust the bunch of them and fulfill the mission the Alliance wanted me to complete? No court would convict them, anyway. And who would I turn over to the authorities, Deep Blue and Polly? And what was the charge? Conspiring to take over the word? As far as I knew the devil was already in charge of the world. And how could I take them into custody when I was the one imprisoned? And there wasn't a chance in hell I could take the devil in for questioning.

"Here we are," they said.

"Thanks, Bill," I said.

"Now there's no need to be rude, Joe," Grace said. "Just because they are evil doesn't mean we shouldn't bless them."

"Bless you, Bill," I said.

"That's Deep Blue to you," they said. "And just because you're on the road to anti-Christ power and authority doesn't mean it is okay to demean your underlings. We have principles here."

"Sorry, Deep, I've got a lot to process. I'm trying to adjust to my new position, and if my attitude offends you, try to understand that the transition from Christian detective to anti-Christ is not an easy one to make."

"We don't do forgiveness here," they said, "but I understand where you're coming from."

"If you're going to keep us in this dingy room," Grace said, "could you at least furnish it with a table and chairs? And the Internet password would be helpful, too."

"I'll see what I can do about the furniture. And the password is 6hellishome66, all lower case. Easy on the data. There are a lot of users down here."

"What's next on the agenda?" I said.

"Your training comes next, as Polly mentioned. But he, as usual, was overly dramatic. Not a criticism. In fact, it's not really an intensive program, and it won't take that long, either. We have designed medical short cuts that will greatly increase your signs and wonders ability, and not only that the process will be accomplished in a reduced amount of time."

"I hope they're not dangerous methods," Grace said.

Grace's concern warmed my heart.

"No, not really. We've adapted AI-controlled plasma and tachyon energy healing pods to suit our needs. You might have already heard about them as MedBeds."

Abner got another one right.

"I've heard of them," Grace said. "My dad has one on order. The best ones cost a fortune. Dad says the beds will diagnose and heal any disease and even reverse aging."

"Bravo," they said. "But the modifications we have made will also allow power to be instilled into Joe's being, so that power to heal will be released at his will. Another fun feature will be the ability to release lightning bolts on a whim. And if that isn't enough, another system component will enable him to receive sufficient hyperspace energy to pull his body, at any given time, out of this dimension long enough for him to walk through solid objects. A need trick, don't you think? So, as you see, Joe, you will be a very well-equipped anti-Christ. Sounds like fun, doesn't it?"

With that Bill left the room, and we heard the key turn in the lock.

"Is there anyone you think we should text or e-mail?" Grace said.

"They've got us monitored," I said. "Otherwise, they wouldn't have returned our phones. Besides, what would my message be? If I text the Alliance, the devil will suspect that we're betraying his cause. If I text Abner and Alfred, they'll be unhappy to know I've left them out in the cold. How about you?"

"I could phone my dad and mom, but they

would be worried sick to know I'm with you in hell planning to be the anti-Christ's bride."

"I'm beginning to suspect we're a long way above deep hell and Satan's pit. Have you noticed this cell stays at a comfortable room temperature? I've never read in the Bible that Hades had air conditioning."

"They didn't have AC back then when scripture was written, so how would they know one way or another?"

"That makes sense."

That made no sense at all, but I knew there were concessions you had to make to maintain on good terms with your spouse, so I thought I might as well start now.

"What makes you think this cell isn't bugged?" Grace said. "They might already think we're Alliance undercover agents?"

I had checked the room for listening devices when we first arrived, but I might have missed some. And even though they weren't treating us now like we were the enemy, I decided I still needed to guard my words.

"Why mention the Alliance?" I said. "You saw my family tree. I'm demon seed through and through, and it's my destiny to rule the world."

I winked at Grace, and she winked back.

"I know it's your destiny, and I'm so privileged to have been chosen to be your mate. I can't tell you how blessed I feel."

"Blessed?"

"I mean, how wonderfully cursed I am to be here with you."

"I can't wait to be imbued with power from one of those converted MedBeds. Imagine how thrilling it would be if I could walk out of here right through that closed door."

"Yes, thrilling, but you wouldn't leave me here alone, would you, Joe?"

"No, of course not, Grace. Don't ever think such a thing. You're my life partner, and where I go you will go, and whatever I face, you will face, for good or ill, in happiness or sadness, come riches or poverty...."

Grace frowned. I consoled her with a wink. She appeared to be weighing up whether she would wink back or not, when we heard the key turn in the lock. The door opened and two armed goons with Bill in the rear shoved Abner and Alfred into our cell and then closed the door. The key turned again in the lock.

"We found these two snooping around," they yelled through the door. "Maybe you can explain to them the situation, and that you are here willingly."

"Well, ain't you two love birds in a fine mess," Abner said. "We let you go off on your own and this is where you end up, locked in a cell thinkin' you're in hell."

"No need to rub it in," Alfred said. "Why don't we instead focus on getting them and us out of here?"

"We're not leaving," I said. "We're on a mission."

Grace nudged me.

"What I mean is we're being groomed to take

over the world. And what are you doing here?"

"We wanted to make sure you weren't going to get into any more trouble," Alfred said.

"We tracked yer phone," Abner added. "And now that we have seen the mess you're in, we need to be gettin' outta here. We can't just stand around here in this broom closet waitin' fer the tribulation."

"I did ask for them to send in a table and chairs," Grace said.

"This ain't no time to be playin' bridge," Abner said.

"Do you know where you are?" Alfred said.

"No, I was drugged, and then I woke up here," I said.

Grace nodded.

"You're in some kind of a storage room in the Ramada Inn downtown," Alfred said.

"Tricky," I said. "What great camouflage, having rooms a few levels above hell."

"No need to be so critical, Joe," Grace said. "It's a fairly good hotel. In fact, my dad owns shares in the company."

"This is getting us nowhere," Alfred said. "I don't know what they told you, but whatever it is they're just setting you up for something."

"You're right," Grace said. "They're setting up Joe to be the anti-Christ. And if he chooses to be the anti-Christ, he will be the best one ever."

"I can't take anymore of this," Abner said. "Call room service and get us out of here."

"You're right," Alfred said. "Let him learn the

hard way."

"You won't regret this," Grace said.

Abner and Alfred searched Grace for meaning, shrugged their shoulders, and gave me a sympathetic look. I rationalized that her illogical statement at least meant something to her.

"Let us outta here," Abner yelled at the door. "They're all yers."

The key turned in the lock, and Bill and the goons waved them out.

"See you when it's over," Alfred said. "We'll hold the fort until then."

"Thank you for your understanding," I said. "And I'll see to it that you have exalted positions in the New World Order."

"Fat chance," Abner said. "You'll be lucky even to have a detective agency after this."

CHAPTER TWENTY-THREE

Polly called us in for another consultation. The flames and the temperature in his lair had been lowered, and he invited us to sit on the now cold rocks. I'd been wondering if my MedBed treatment was next on the agenda, but Polly seemed to be glum and had other things on his mind.

"I don't mind telling you," he said. "We've had a bit of a setback."

"Oh, dear," Grace said. "Nothing too dire I hope."

"Well, I'm sorry to say we've had some financial challenges. Some of this new technology has put a strain on our world domination budget, not to mention increases in salaries and building rental. The Boss has an enormous underground empire, as you might imagine, and he has a lot of expenses to cover. And sadly, our MedBed is out of commission for the moment. Our power imbuing modifications exerted a strain on its primary circuits and it blew a gasket. We're working now to have it repaired. The main challenge is getting a qualified technician to come here and fix it. Not many know about lightning bolt creation and walking through walls technology. And some when they hear where we are located are leery about coming so close to hell."

"But isn't this a Ramada Inn?" Grace said.

"True, my dear, but this hotel actually sits on a major Pacific Northwest gate that goes straight down to hell."

"Okay, I get it," I said. "So what's the plan now?"

"We're needing to do a bit of a fund raiser. And since you are the anti-Christ in waiting, you are heavily invested now in the outcome of our project to subdue the world for Satan, so any ideas you might have would be appreciated."

"I could ask my dad," Grace said. "He has billions, and I'm sure he would help me as long as I didn't tell him what it's for. How about you, Joe? You and your family are very well off."

I was beginning to smell a rat. Not the kind of rat that came right up and bit you on the nose, but the kind that lurked in the dark waiting for the best moment to scurry into your larder and nibble on the cheese.

"I suppose I could contribute to the cause," I said. "No need to ask my family. I've got plenty."

"Splendid," Polly said. "We should have everything up and running in no time. We only need a million or two."

"Oh, is that all," Grace said. "I've got that much in the account my daddy set up for me. And what about you, Joe? When we're married, our finances will all be shared, anyway."

"Sure, money was never what I was in this game for. If a couple of million are all it takes to grease the wheel, then I'm in."

"Oh, Joe, isn't this fun?"

"Your cooperation in this matter has already been duly noted by the Boss," Polly said. "And your generosity will accrue to your benefit in the demonic age to come."

"Do you think we could receive a benefit now?" I said. "For instance, we would like better living conditions instead of that cell. A suite would be preferable. And two connecting bedrooms would be appropriate, since Grace and I have not as yet tied the knot."

"You're so thoughtful, Joe," Grace said.

"This can be arranged," Polly said, "as soon as the funds have been made available for the use of the Great Cause, the cause of all causes, the subjection of the world to the Great Satan and his thousand years reign. You need only transfer the funds to our offshore bank account in the Bahamas."

"Consider it done," Grace said.

"Sure, I'll kick in," I said.

I wasn't so sure, but what was money anyway? You spent your life chasing the do-re-mi, and all it got you in the end was a place to park your carcass down below, under six feet of dirt, the dirt we all rose from. But what in this world did it get you? Not much to speak of. The rich got rich and poor got poorer and everyone looked stupid dead. But life was intended to be more than that. We who knew the score were heading into the great beyond. The big sleep was more than a long snooze of nothingness. It was eternity in spades.... I caught myself just in time. The stress of all that money going down the drain had kicked me into hardboiled mode again.

"Are you okay, Joe?" Grace said. "You look a little pale."

"Just hungry. Do you think you could also send a menu to our suite, Polly? We haven't eaten since we got here. I don't mind fasting, but only if I feel led, and not because of some religious idea that all you've got to do is sacrifice your flesh and presto whatever you wanted was yours."

"I'll get on that right away," Polly said. "And just so you know, we've got a lot of religious folks down there, and they haven't eaten for centuries. Funny, eh?"

I was surprised Polly had a sense of humor, warped as it was.

"That's not fair," Grace said.

"Not our decision," Polly said. "Deep Blue will show you to your rooms now. I trust that you will make the funds transfer upon your arrival there. If not you will be returned to your downgraded accommodation."

"Fair enough," I said.

"Oh, good," Grace said. "Finally! A shower!"

"You still smell good to me," I said.

"Darling Joe, you're so genteel."

CHAPTER TWENTY-FOUR

Once established in our new digs we made the money transfer. Polly had arranged for new sets of clothes to be sent to our suite. We showered and then ordered from the dinner menu, even though we weren't sure what meal we should begin with. We didn't know if the Satanic portal affected time or not. Our phones said dinner time, so that's what we went with. The food was average.

After dinner Grace and I realized we needed a way to communicate with each other without the prying bugs and eyes of the damned clueing in on our conversation. We decided to play tent. Grace grasped my meaning when I gestured toward the bed and whipped off the top quilt. The spies would think we were only getting a little pre-marital frisky. So armed with the flashlights on our phones we erected our tent on my king sized bed. Our heads would function as the tent poles. I stashed two pens and two pads of hotel stationary beneath our makeshift abode. Once inside we giggled a few times for effect and then proceeded to be about the business at hand.

Isn't this fun? Grace wrote.

I could get used to this. I wrote.

We giggled some more. Inside our cozy tent we were oblivious to the seriousness of our predicament, sitting as we were, encamped above a major gate of hell.

We need to have a plan. I wrote.

Granted. Grace wrote.

We giggled again in unison. I was beginning to look forward to marriage even more now. Grace was a whole lot of fun down deep.

Don't worry, when we bust these felons, we'll get our money back. I wrote.

I'm not worried, Joe. What's a few million here or there, anyway? She wrote.

My battary is running low. I wrote.

Spelling, Joe! She chastised.

Busted, I thought. No spellcheck on paper.

I think we need to agree right now that we are on a mission for the Alliance, and that we are in no way tempted to become Mr. and Mrs. anti-Christ. I wrote.

Whatever you say, Joe, I'm easy. She wrote.

I think you need to be more comitted than that. No offence. I wrote.

Spelling again, Joe, two ems in committed, but okay I swear my allegiance to the White Hats. Maybe we should take a blood oath. Did room service leave any dinner cutlery behind? She wrote.

We giggled some more. I wasn't used to giggling. Hardboiled detectives didn't giggle. That was a pretty well established fact, but I was no longer one of those hardnosed types, was I? I was now a literate detective, and spelling, of course, was not a big concern.

Now that we are both agreed and we are on the

same page, we need to find a way to bring the miscreants to the service. I wrote.

That's surface, not service, Joe. No matter. I agree. I know this is your specialty, and I don't mean to step on your professional toes, but I think we need to find a way to disarm their goons and then focus on Deep Blue and especially Apollyon, The Destroyer, aka Polly. We can probably get them for tax evasion. We can save the devil for later. She wrote. *P.S. Although, as I'm sure you know, capturing the devil isn't really scriptural.* She also wrote.

Inciteful. As the Alliance assured us, if we can get Polly and Bill to the surface, they will take over from there.

Be careful of your homonyms, Joe. You mean insightful, not inciteful, which means to set something into motion, like a riot. She wrote.

WHATEVER. I wrote.

I'd lost my giggle.

Sorry, I won't do it again. I hate it when I'm corrected, so I should be sensitive and not correct others, especially you, Joe. Do unto others. She wrote.

Have you noticed it's getting hot under here? I wrote. *Do you think we should put our heads together to make it look like we're engaged in questionable activity under here?*

Oh, Joe, I thought you'd never ask. She wrote.

The hurt I experienced from her critical spirit dissolved in the luscious experience of her squarely planted lips. I tossed my pen and paper, and Grace did the same, but reason and the immediacy of our predicament prevailed, and we threw off our tent.

"We don't want to be a bad witness to whoever might be watching," she said.

"Are you sure it's not whomever?" I said.

"Funny, Joe," she said. "You should exercise your wit more often."

I wasn't in the mood most days to exercise anything, let alone my wit. I wouldn't say I was moody and certainly I wouldn't say I was depressed. I wasn't the depressed type, but I had been starved for affection most of my life. Now here I was sharing a suite with a gorgeous female, who was open to pursuing a deepening relationship with me and was destined to be my partner in life. Meanwhile, I was stuck in a rut trying to save the world. My selfish desires were being sacrificed for the greater good, but I wasn't one to whine.

"We better get some sleep," I said. "I'll see you in the morning, or whatever time of day it is when we wake up."

"You're so wise, Joe," Grace said. "Sleep is what we need right now."

Grace exited my room, her fragrance lingering. Sleep. How was I to sleep when success meant a life of bliss, and failure a life of torment? Marriage. What a prospect. And would six months of once-a-week marriage counseling be required? I didn't know the policy of The Church of the Manifest Presence. And who would marry us? Her pastor or mine? Her mother would come into play, of course, and she would be a controlling force. Grace was an only child, and her parents would no doubt want to finance a marriage event of the century. What would the wedding of a billionaire's daughter look like? I might never know. If the devil discovered my betrayal of everything evil, before I exposed Deep Blue and Polly and their plan to rule the world, then I was doomed. I might never see daylight again. And then the prospect of uniting with Grace, the lovely, would fade into a distant dream, as my life drained away, skewered by Satan's pitchfork and choked under the stifling weight of his dark soul. That was my last thought, as my life's troubles slipped into a deep chasm, succumbing to my weary mind and body's demand for silence.

CHAPTER TWENTY-FIVE

My head felt like it had been hit by a truck. I had a hangover. A giggle hangover. I not only had giggled, I had giggled a lot. And I wrote things I shouldn't have written. I wasn't a giggler. Little girls giggled. No self-respecting private detective giggled.

Grace sprang through our adjoining door like an angel on the loose, her sunshine yellow dressing gown flowing, as if enlivened by her being. I was barely awake and in my delicate condition her entrance stunned me. Coffee was on the way.

"Morning, Joe," she said. "It's a great day to be alive, don't you think?"

I wasn't yet awake enough to think. Room service knocked on the door. I let her in. She wheeled her cart in, set the tray on the table, and wheeled out. I was short on tip money.

"I'm sorry," I said to Grace. "I should have ordered you something."

"Oh, heavens no. I ate ages ago. I was patient because I knew that you needed your sleep, so I did my morning devotional while was waiting for you to wake up. I feel so wonderfully refreshed, and I have a strong feeling this is going to be a big day."

I tried to match her enthusiasm but could only muster up a grunt. I sipped my black coffee and wondered how she could do her devotional without a Bible.

"How could you do a devotional without scripture?" I said.

"From memory," she said.

Figures," I said.

What does that mean, Joe?"

I sipped some more coffee, eyed my poached egg on toast, and sensed we were about to have our first fight.

"Do you think it was wise to do your devotional? You do remember where we are?"

"It was all in my head," she said. "Who would know?"

"When we take up our anti-Christ positions of authority, there will be no more devotionals, unless they are exalting our leader, the Great Satan."

"I see what you're saying. It's hard to break old habits, but in the future I'll try to remember who we are and where we are. May I sit with you while you eat breakfast, Joe?"

"Suit yourself."

"Suit yourself? What has happened to you, Joe? You weren't like this last night."

"It takes me a while to wake up, that's all. I'm not fresh as a daisy first thing in the morning like some people around here."

"Joe! You need to apologize, whether you are slow to wake up or not."

"You're right. I'm sorry. I'm probably suffering the effects of being in such close proximity to hell."

"That's okay. I know the strain you're under. But we need to stick together, or who knows what might happen?"

I decided to tell her.

"I'm embarrassed about giggling so much last night," I said.

"Oh, no, don't be. Laughter is good for you, Joe."

"Laughter is one thing, but giggling is something else. And not only that, giggling triggered a dream."

"What kind of dream, Joe? A bad dream?"

"It wasn't good. I dreamed I was lost in hell and there was a demon assigned to me whose only job was to tickle me with a crow's feather for all eternity. I was condemned to giggle forever. And it wasn't a healthy giggle, either. It was a sinister giggle, like I was giggling at being in hell. And then I woke up feeling creepy under my chin."

"Oh, that's horrible," Grace said. "But look at me, Joe. I'm right here with you now, and you need not giggle ever again."

"Thank you for listening," I said.

"That's what I'm here for, Joe. And don't think there isn't anything you can't tell me."

I understood her meaning, so I wasn't going to draw attention to her triple negative. Right now, I needed to reflect on who I was at my core. There was no doubt my superfluous giggling was an indication that I was in an identity transition. The giggles were simply an indication of some minor personality fragmentation. The result was my bad attitude towards Grace. But so what if I had been moody. Changes in identity weren't easy. I had to go easy on myself. And I certainly wasn't depressed. And if I had to give up the PI game altogether that was the price I would have to pay for integrity. But then who would I be? And then what about Grace? How would she relate to whoever I became? Relationships were hard at the best of times, and when personal histories were not revealed, then they might easily come back to haunt in the future. My history was the perfect example. I was raised by my aunt, who I thought was my mother, because my real mother, my aunt's sister, left me with her sister all those years, so she could marry rich and live rich and think rich, while I spent thirty odd years wondering who my father was, and thinking my first mother was my mother, who, as it turned out was really my aunt, and my dad who was dead in my mind showed up alive, the whole time not knowing I existed, because my real mother, who was now my second mother in my mind, hadn't told him either, so she could live the good life, rich and happy, in the American way. But even though she had deserted me, she was not short on generosity now. She'd given me enough do-re-mi to set me up in a dozen private eye offices, in a dozen penthouse apartments in a dozen towns. There was no price on guilt. But having all those greenbacks took a little getting used to. I was loaded now, and all that money was nothing to giggle at. I pulled myself together and poked at my poached egg.

"Where did you go, Joe? You're such a deep

thinker. I wish you would let me in more."

"Sometimes things are better left unsaid."

I could see no reason to let her in on the details until sometime after we were wed.

"Do you think we'll need pre-marriage counseling, Joe?" Grace said.

"That wouldn't be wise anytime soon," I said.

"Do you think we should discuss our current state and plan our day," Grace said and winked.

"I'm not playing tent again, if that's what you mean."

CHAPTER TWENTY-SIX

The door knocker sounded. I left my egg to ooze its yellow yolk, its stare evoking in me feelings of guilt, and got up to look through the peep hole. A middle-aged man in a hotel uniform was at the door.

"State your business," I said.

"Might I have a few words with you, sir," he said.

I opened the door and he stepped in with the air of a professional host.

"What can I do for you?" I said.

I hoped I didn't sound rude. But we already had enough going on without being harassed by the hired help.

"There's a small matter of the bill," he said.

"Bill for what?" I said.

"Well, for the suite, sir."

"You'll have to talk to Deep Blue or Apollyon about that. We're their guests."

"I'm sorry, sir, but I'm not acquainted with the people of whom you speak."

"Well, how was the suite booked, then?"

"The suite wasn't exactly booked, sir. In fact you seem to have occupied our hotel premises without going through proper channels."

"But Deep Blue and Polly let us in."

"I'm sorry, sir, but if you would be kind enough to make payment arrangements with us then we would be pleased to forgo the need to have the authorities involved."

"But we had room service," I said.

"Yes, we have talked to our staff about that, and, in fact, that is what led us to the realization we had unregistered guests in this suite."

"Oh, dear," Grace said.

I didn't see that coming. The penny dropped, and it dropped hard. My anti-Christ aspirations and any possibility of apprehending the One Worlders, not to mention recovering our money, had gone down the drain of despair. But I would be a man about it. After all, Grace was there. And she would be watching how I might behave in such trying circumstances.

"I would be happy to pay for the suite," I said. "And I do apologize for any inconvenience I might have caused you and this fine establishment. We have enjoyed our stay here, and we will work out our differences with Deep Blue and Polly ourselves, so you need not be concerned any further."

"Thank you, sir. If you would then inform the front desk as soon as possible of your credit card details, we will consider the matter closed. And as you no doubt know, check-out time is 11:00 a.m. Good day."

He left us to consider our next move. I realized that searching the hotel would be of no use. They would have checked out by now, if they had ever checked in. Hmm, the cell would have been easy enough for them to fake, and the theater would have been a little more challenging. But the fake hell room was a masterpiece. So whoever they were, and whatever their motives, they were professionals.

"It's not your fault, Joe," Grace said. "They were experts in their field."

"But were they the real thing, or were they only con artists?"

"They did seem like they were minions of Satan," Grace said.

"Yes, very curious. Who would have guessed?"

"That's right, Joe. They were as clever at deception as Tom Cruise in those Mission Impossible movies."

"Those are just movies, and besides, he's a Scientologist."

"No need to be judgmental, Joe. Some people aren't as blessed as we are to know the truth."

"I guess we'd better get out of here. At least they bought us some new clothes."

"My guess is they will be an additional item on our hotel bill," Grace said.

"Abner and Alfred are going to love this."

"You did your best, Joe, and that's all a person can do. Their judgments are of no consequence."

"This whole thing doesn't add up. I can't help but think we missed something. There was more to this than we are aware of right now."

"It's reassuring to think so. But look at us. We have our whole lives to look forward to, Joe. The best is yet to come. We were born for such a time as this.

The world is our oyster. We don't need to be burying our lives in the underground filth the devil is trying to splatter the world with. Let the Alliance take care of it. They are equipped for that kind of work. Let's get as far away from Satan as we possibly can. I don't know why they chose you anyway, Joe."

"It just doesn't add up. But if good men do nothing, the enemy will triumph. Who is going to stop the foul demons unless the people of the world stand-up and be counted?"

"You're so deep, Joe. That's why the Alliance chose you. You're a White Hat all the way."

"And you're a White Bonnet, Grace."

"That's the nicest thing you've ever said to me, Joe. I think we are going to make our mark in the world, no matter what we choose to do. And we will do it together."

It was settled. Our future was secure, except for the devil's incessant plan to rule the world and to be worshipped by all those who were left after the Rapture. But no matter what Grace said, I needed to continue the battle on the front lines.

"This isn't over," I said, and I didn't care who heard me say it.

"You're so brave, Joe. I don't know what my life would have been without you."

She was scaring me now. But I had to move ever forward into the unknown, and of course, into some of the known also. Life was here to take hold of, and I needed to be courageous and take hold of it with both hands.

The phone rang. The front desk wanted to know if we were going to vacate the suite any time soon, and would we mind stopping by downstairs to settle up. Yes, it was time to go and time to step into our future.

CHAPTER TWENTY-SEVEN

"You missed Christmas," Abner said. "On purpose probably, so ya wouldn't hafta have a staff party."

"I'm glad you're happy to see me, Abner," I said.

"We are happy you came to your senses," Alfred said. "And that you're none the worse for wear."

There was no need to tell them about the money issue. The money was gone, and that was that. It was what it was.

"What kinda scheme were they tryin' to get you involved in, anyway?" Abner said. "Somethin' about being the anti-Christ or somethin'?"

"No need to go into that," I said. "We have more important things to discuss."

"Like what?" Alfred said. "We don't even have a client right now."

"Ya, like what?" Abner said. "Yer lady friend was our only client, and you've been takin' care of her real personal like, haven't ya? Hangin' out on a bunk bed in a broom closet, real cozy like."

"Thanks for the summary, Abner," I said. "But that was completely innocent and all in the line of duty."

"Did ya hear that, Alfred, he calls his mating adventure all in the line of duty?"

"Leave him alone," Alfred said. "Right now we need to do something about attracting new clients."

"Why don't we take out an ad in the Personals under Casanova fer hire?" Abner said. "Or how about, anti-Christ available fer small parties."

"You're not being helpful, Abner," Alfred said.

"Okay, fine, I deserve it," I said. "But now let's move on."

The intercom buzzed.

"She's here," Pen said.

"Send her in," I said.

"Who?" she said.

"You didn't tell me who."

"No, I didn't, and by the way, thanks for the joy-filled staff party."

Grace entered. She was wearing a frown. I didn't like the looks of this. I liked the looks of her, but it didn't like the looks of her frown. It meant something deep was going on. For a woman like her to be wearing one was a bad sign. She was happy and cheerful most of the time, but not now. No she wasn't. She plunked herself in my client's chair.

"Are you okay?" I said.

"No, not really. My parents are unhappy with me. They are suggesting that I get a job."

"What brought that on?" I said.

"They are not altogether happy with my choice of mate, and they want me to be independent. They don't want me to be relying on their money, either, or on my future husband's prospects."

"Wise parents," Abner said.

"I was wondering if you might need some help around here," she said.

"Hey, there's an idea," Abner said. "Alfred and I can retire, and you two can go into the PI business together. What do you say, Alfred, have you had enough of sleuthin'?"

Alfred's response was interrupted by a knock at the door. I buzzed Pen.

"She pushed her way passed me," Pen said. "I don't know what she wants."

Abner got up and opened the door. A woman about 30-years-old entered. She was wearing mink. I wondered if she was looking for protection from PETA. She had blonde hair, a pallid complexion, and wore a big red collagen smile. Grace gave her the once over and shrugged.

"What can we do for you?" I said. "I'm Joe LaFlam."

"These are your partners, I take it," she said, giving Abner and Alfred a nod. "And she is your what?"

"This is Grace, my soon-to-be bride."

"Cozy," she said. "I'm Darla. Do you mind if I sit?"

I smiled at Grace and she vacated my client's chair.

"This should be good," Abner said. "I can hardly wait to hear what Darla has to say."

"Cool it," Alfred said.

"The reason I'm here is to ask you to do a job for me," Darla said. "Forgive me for barging in like that, but this is urgent. I need you to liberate my husband from a criminal gang before something really bad happens. I can't go to the police, for obvious reasons."

"What's the gang's M.O.?"

"M.O.?"

"Yeah, you know, their modus operandi. What's their gig?"

"Oh, I see," she said. "As far as I know they prey on unsuspecting Christians. The leader of the gang calls himself Apollyon, or something like that. I've overheard my husband on the phone call him Polly."

"Hmm, interesting," I said.

Grace rolled her winkless eyes at me.

"Do you know where we can find Polly and the gang right now?" I said.

"Their main hang out is in the back room of a local bar on Main Street, south of Kingsway, called Lucky Lucy's. I need someone to talk some sense into him. This can't go on. There's no denying that he is an excellent provider, but I can't in good conscience continue to live off the proceeds of his criminal activity."

She took a tissue from her purse and dabbed her left teary eye with it and then tidied her pretty little nose.

"I see," I said. "Yes, there are some confidence schemes that can be quite profitable."

Alfred and Abner's interest began to be piqued, and Grace gave me a do something look. I needed to steer my partners away from the obvious.

"Our fees are quite reasonable," I said.

"Cost is no object," Darla said. "I can pay you quite well. He just deposited a sizeable amount into my account. He likes to keep me well supplied."

"Well, the money won't go to waste with us," I said.

"Anything to get Bill out of this racket, so he doesn't go to jail," she said.

"Say, I thought I heard those goons call...." Alfred said.

"Ya, that's right," Abner said.

"No need to go into that," I said. "We can examine various aspects of the case later."

"You will do it, then?" Darla said.

I surveyed the room. "What do you say?" I said.

Alfred and Abner nodded. Grace gave me a covert wink.

"Yes, of course," I said. "We will be happy to take your case, and we will make every effort to liberate your husband from the nefarious hands of Apollyon."

"Oh, joy," Abner said. "I can hardly wait."

CHAPTER TWENTY-EIGHT

Grace and I drove down Main Street. Alfred and Abner followed. The falling rain was turning to sleet. The traffic was heavy. The post Christmas shoppers were out in full force. We had a job to do. Sure, we were stepping on the toes of the police department, but what PI worth his salt didn't? Besides, we had some personal business to attend to, if and when we caught up with Polly.

"Watch out for that woman in the crosswalk," Grace said.

"No worries," I said.

We weren't even married yet, and she was already telling me how to drive. And now it looked like she wanted to partner up with me in the PI business. Where was all this headed?

"There it is," she said, "Lucky Lucy's on the right. Pull over. There's a spot behind that taxi."

I pulled over. There was no sense bucking her order since she was right. Alfred and Abner passed us. They were headed around the back, to prevent the gang from making their escape into the alley. We were all packing rods, except for Grace. She was to stay in the car until we established the gang's whereabouts. I exited my vehicle, and Grace said she was coming, too. I should have known. I knew better than to argue.

Lucky Lucy's was a dive of the worst kind. The sign hung askew on a chain under the ripped awning. The windows were foggy, probably caused by rotting insulation. The bar itself looked like it was rotting, the perfect hangout for Polly and his gang.

Inside, a few patrons on barstools gave us sidelong sneers as we entered. The bartender was an elderly blonde hussy in need of a denturist. Over at the pool table a couple observed our entrance. Her eyes were blank and cold. She was wearing a guy to match. He was draped over her, like he had no life on his own. They disentangled. "Your shot," she said.

"Is Polly here?" I said to the bartender.

"Who wants to know?" she said.

I could see there was a door at the far end of the bar beside the men's washroom.

"He in there?" I said, pointing.

"Maybe," she said. "Are you going to order something, or are you just here to be a nuisance?"

I tossed a fifty on the bar and headed for the door.

"Hold that till we get back," I said.

The door wasn't locked. I opened it and stepped in. There was a poker game in progress. Five gamblers were huddled under a hanging lamp, their cards and poker chips arranged on the green felt table cloth.

"Hey, close that door," yelled a man wearing an eyeshade. "And who let you in here?"

"Where's Polly?" I said.

"Who?" the man said.

"Apollyon," I said.

"Never heard of him," he said. "Now get out of here and take that babe with you."

Alfred and Abner then appeared out of nowhere.

"And how did you two get in here?" the man said. "This isn't an open house party."

"We didn't see anyone come out the back exit," Alfred said to me.

The poker players were getting jumpy. I needed to make a move. I stepped over to the table and flipped it over. The cards and chips went flying. The gamblers were not amused. Sure enough, there was a trap door under the table.

"We came armed," I said, "so all of you back away."

The gamblers began to scoop their chips off the floor and to vacate the premises. I was happy there was no resistance. The green eyeshade was last to leave.

"You're going to pay big time for this," he said. "We have friends in high places."

"You mean in low places, don't you?" I said.

He slammed the door on the way out, and I lifted the trap door. An eerie red glow radiated from the opening and shone into the room.

"Ya got somethin' right for a change," Abner said.

"It was just a hunch," I said.

"I don't think we should go down there, Joe," Grace said. "Who knows what we will find?"

"We didn't come here fer nothin'," Abner said. "I

want to know what's goin' on down there."

"I'm the one going down," I said.

"I'm going, too," Grace said. "I've got as much interest in this as you, Joe, and you know what I mean."

"What does she mean?" Alfred said.

"We'll get to that later," I said. "Right now I want you and Abner to stay up here and guard this hole until we get back. There might be some opposition coming, and I don't want us to get sealed off down there."

"Whatever you say, boss," Abner said.

Abner sounded sincere. I wondered if he was having a bad day.

Squinting through the red glare, I could see there was a ladder, and its base rested on the floor about 10-feet below.

"Okay, down I go," I said.

"Break a leg," Abner said.

"You're so brave, Joe," Grace said. "I'll be right behind you."

I decided not to comment on the fact that she was just as brave. She was a strange woman, and I knew our life together would be a very special time of surprises, triumphs and failures, as we reaped the spoils of lives well lived. That is if we survived our current confrontation with Polly, who for all we knew was waiting….

"Well, get going," Alfred said.

"Ya, stop stalling," Abner said. "We haven't got all day."

The descent was uneventful. Grace followed, and I caught her in an embrace at the foot of the ladder, for no other reason than I could. Funny what one does in the face of danger and possible death.

"What's that?" Grace said.

"What's what," I said.

"That...over in the corner. It looks like a safe."

"You're right. I wonder if it belongs to Polly."

"You've got that right," a familiar voice said. "You just wouldn't leave well enough alone, would you? What's a few million bucks to people like you, anyway?"

Polly emerged from the red shadows, menacing us with his familiar cobra sceptre.

"We didn't come for the money," I said. "We're looking for Bill, aka Deep Blue. We're doing a job for a client."

"So it's Darla, isn't it? She's at it again." he said. "She's become a liability. We've got a good thing going, and all she wants to do is rescue Bill and take him back to his old life of washing dishes in a restaurant."

"What do you mean?" Grace said. "That we didn't come for the money?"

"There's no price on honesty, Polly," I said. "But you wouldn't understand that, would you? And by the way, what are you doing in this hole?"

"You don't get it do you," Polly said. "You think this is all about the money. There's more going on here than is dreamed of in your little world."

"Try me," I said. "And have you got somewhere for us to sit down. This whole affair has been tiring and stressful."

"What a wimp. But after I tell you what is really going on you're going to need to sit down. And my name's not Polly, it's Ralph. The real Apollyon is busy far below."

Ralph led us into another room where a few discarded beer kegs stood. We each sat down on one. They proved to be more comfortable than the brimstone rocks.

"Okay, so what's the score?" I said.

"Is there a game on?" Grace said. "Where's the TV?"

"No," I said, "that's just an expression. It means in this case, what's this all about, Ralph?"

"Oh, I see. You can be so mysterious sometimes, Joe. I hope one day I can come to understand the workings of your mind."

I hoped I would, too.

"Are you two done?" Ralph said. "This is how it all works."

"All what works?" I said.

"I was about to tell you that, if you would just listen."

"Okay, we're listening," I said.

"You're sure?"

"Yes."

"Okay, this is how it works. We're allowed to engage in our con game as long as we conform to certain obligations that the Boss has sworn us to."

"What boss," I said. "You don't mean Lucy, do you?

"Lucy is real, but of course he doesn't really like to be called that. You might have noticed we had some supernatural help in our little con game. There were a few time-warp effects for instance, courtesy of the Boss, and then there was the pit of hell special effect. The Boss helps us to succeed in what we like to call our business, as long as we hold up our end of the bargain in the end.

"You mean," Grace said. "You mean, you sold your souls to the devil?"

"He's not so bad," Ralph said.

"Then why are you hiding out down here?" I said. "You should be out spending your ill-gotten gain, travelling the world, seeing the sights, lying in the sun."

"We've gotten used to living in the dark. Habits are hard to break. We enjoy our work more than spending the money. You have to admit we did an outstanding job of deceiving you, didn't we? That's our reward. An evil job well done."

Ralph made an attempt to laugh. A labored wheeze was the result.

"I must say I do like the red lighting," Grace said, in an attempt, it seemed, to encourage Ralph. "It adds to the mystery of the place."

"Oh, thank-you for saying so," Ralph said.

"Okay, so what about the Spelunkers?" I said. "Are they for real?"

"Absolutely," Ralph said. "You should know that. But you'll never catch them. The Alliance won't either. The Boss told us all about the Alliance. He plans to take them down and the whole Q nonsense with them."

"What about the quantum computers? The one the Alliance has is fifth generation. That beats anything the devil has."

"You're kidding," Ralph said. "You really don't know what's going on, do you? The Boss invented quantum computers, and he provides the users with what they need to know. Anytime it suits him he can lead the Alliance down the garden path, and he does. The computers are just a complex Ouija Board."

If what Ralph said was true, Abner was right again.

"What about all that other stuff you told us about? The Illuminati, and HAARP and DARPA, and what about the Reptilians?"

"All factual. The Boss is the head Reptilian."

"What about my genealogy and the anti-Christ offer you gave me?"

"We faked your anti-Christ eligibility, of course. You aren't the anti-Christ type."

I was thankful for that.

"Oh, Joe," Grace said. "I didn't believe it for a minute. They wouldn't be able to change you no matter how powerful the converted MedBeds might be."

"The Boss doesn't need MedBeds, either. He converts power when he needs to, when it serves his ultimate goal. He'll be ruling the world soon. And you Christians can't do anything about it, either."

"Are you forgetting our Boss?" I said.

"We don't talk about Him. It's not healthy."

"Is Bill around? We'd like to have a word with him. We need to fulfill our obligation to our client."

"It won't do you any good. Bill is bought and paid for. But if you want to hear it for yourself, I'll get him."

Ralph left the room and came back a few minutes later with Bill in tow. We asked him the pertinent questions, and Ralph was right. Bill was a lifer in the devil's kingdom.

"I've got no life out there," Bill said. "Darla will have to finally understand that. You tell her that for me, and also let her know the financial support will continue."

"Ironic," Grace said.

"I agree," I said.

"How's that?" Ralph and Bill said.

"She'll be paying for our services with our money," I said.

"Funny," Ralph and Bill said.

"You wouldn't think about opening your safe, I suppose," I said.

"No chance," Ralph said. "We earned your money fair and square."

"Let's go, Joe," Grace said. "There's no point in carrying on with this any further."

"That's right. Go live your lives," Ralph said. "And don't come back here again. The Boss is losing patience with you as it is. Our con game is nothing compared to what's happening deeper down. Down there the minions get meaner, and I advise you not to try to go there. You might consider our little interaction as mild entertainment compared to what's down below."

"You could walk out of here with us," Grace said. "You don't have to serve the devil."

"There's only jail for us out there, and after that the Boss would claim what's his."

"Your souls could still be saved," Grace said. "It's never too late."

"It is for us," Ralph said.

"Okay, we're out of here," I said. "But remember Grace is right. It is never too late."

"You Christians are all the same," Ralph said. "You never take no for an answer."

"Let's go, Joe. I'm getting cold down here."

"Ironic," I said.

"What's ironic, Joe? Oh, I get it. Cold in the heat of hell. You're so funny. In the face of it all, you can pause a moment to provide a chuckle or two for those who have no hope."

"Like I said, get out of here," Ralph said.

Grace and I said our goodbyes to Ralph and Bill, two con artists bound for hell, and then we climbed the ladder to freedom. Alfred and Abner were waiting for us, guarding the hole. They had taken residence in two of the vacated gamblers' chairs and were engaged in a competition of tossing cards into Alfred's fedora.

"Did you miss us?" I said.

"What did you find out," Alfred said. "Did you find Bill?"

"Yes, but Bill won't be coming with us," I said.

"Did those swindlers give ya yer money back?" Abner said.

"What makes you think they have any of our money?" I said.

"Alfred and I can put two and two together. How much was it?"

"It's time to leave," I said, "before there's trouble. We can talk about any outstanding issues at a later date."

"Quite a tidy sum, eh?" Abner said. "Figures."

CHAPTER TWENTY-NINE

Grace and I sped onward in my Bentley, the winter streets slimed by the sloshing sleet. We were headed for my penthouse, where we could freshen up before we went to dinner, and where we could continue our courtship without the strains of PI work burdening us with its cares. I answered my hands-free calling as I changed lanes. A disgruntled motorist honked. The unmistakeable gruff voice on the other end of the line didn't sound pleased.

"So where have you been," Leo said.

"Don't you know?" I said. "I thought your quantum computer knew everything."

"Still the smart guy, eh? Well, the boss has been wanting to know about our progress, and I mean the big boss."

Grace shouted, "Whoa, that yellow light just turned red...."

"We've had a few problems with a big boss of our own for the past few days," I said. "So, what do you want us to do about your current problems?"

"Look out for that cyclist, Joe," Grace said. "She's sliding in the slush."

"And why did you let us get hijacked?" I said. "You were late for our Little Mountain appointment, for what reason?"

"We're sorry for that," Leo said. "It couldn't be helped."

"What, did your computer come down with dementia?"

"Like I said, it couldn't be helped, smart guy. We were attacked on another front."

"Watch out, Joe, you're straddling the line," Grace said.

"Well, what can we do for you now," I said. "We're all ears."

"Q+ wants to see some results. We're under the gun. And we need you to do a deep dive to get us some information."

"I don't like the sound of deep dive. I've had enough deep dive experience for a while."

"You tell him, Joe," Grace said. "Oops, look out for that beer truck...."

"You probably know that I'm not the kind of PI that backs away from a case, but most of the felons we've encountered so far are only the tip of the iceberg."

"Iceberg, Joe?" Grace said.

"Right, we were merely licked and tickled by insignificant purveyors of hell's flames."

"Much better," Grace said.

"We know how much money you lost," Leo said, and I'm offering you the opportunity to get it back, as a bonus for doing us a service."

"Ralph's not going to give it back," Grace said. "Oops, look out for that woman, you just went through a crosswalk, and she just made an unkind gesture, Joe."

"I saw her in the rearview," I said. "Some people's manners. She should have been watching where she was going."

"Are you still there?" Leo said.

"What's the offer this time?" I said.

"We'll compensate you for your losses. Forget about Ralph, whoever he is, and we'll pay you for your services. The Alliance has unlimited resources."

"Why were you so cheap the first time around then?" I said.

"There's the entrance to your garage," Grace said.

"I know where my building is," I said.

I turned in without incident, and left Leo hanging. The cell signal was lost in the underground parking garage until the building's signal booster kicked in. I pulled into my parking stall.

"Are you still there?" Leo said.

"We're here, and we will always be here when duty calls and the freedom of the world is at stake. What else can a person do? Sure, a person might want to run off and hide, so they can save their skin, but what does that say about their commitment to the next generation and the generations after that, unless, of course, the Lord comes back in the meantime, and then He would do the saving, and He would put the devil in the place where he belongs until His thousand years' reign ended, and after that the devil would be released for a short time ...."

"Do you mind," Leo said. "We don't have time

for a study of the Book of Revelations."

"It's Revelation, not Revelations," I said. "Why does everyone want to add an "s"?"

"Whatever," Leo said.

"You're so clever, Joe," Grace said. "Our children are going to learn so much from you."

"When and where do you want to meet?" I said. "I don't suppose you want the whole world knowing what the plan is, do you?"

"I'll meet you in your office in five minutes," Leo said.

"You can't be far away then," I said.

"I'm in your office now. It'll take you about five minutes to get up here."

"How did you get into my office? Oh, never mind. We'll be right up."

Pen must have been on one of her extended coffee breaks.

"Do you trust them, Joe?"

Who could you trust these days? But I said I would finish the case, whatever that might mean, and that's exactly what I was going to do, no matter what.

"Who can you trust these days?" I said.

"You can trust me, Joe. That you can be sure of."

CHAPTER THIRTY

Grace was pensive on our trip up. I was lost in a fog of uncertainty. Not about the mission, but about Grace. Was she the one for me? She seemed to think so. In fact, she knew so. But could I go along with that? I tried to look past the fact that she smelled so good, and with my discerning eyes I tried to penetrate deep into her heart.

"What are you looking at, Joe?"

It was no use. She was impenetrable, even for me, a seasoned detective. I decided the best thing to do was put my trust in her smell and the fact that she had chosen me. A life of marital bliss or a lamb to the slaughter? Only time would tell.

"Will you marry me?" I said.

"Yes, oh yes! Oh, Joe, I thought you'd never ask. We are the happiest people alive!"

We embraced in a divine embrace, the elevator heading up to our future together.

"Let's elope," Grace said. "Let's runaway now. Leo can wait. And my family would only make a big fuss about the whole thing anyway."

"What about pre-marital counselling?" I said.

"Forget about that, Joe. We know about finances and the birds and bees, don't we?"

"Yes, I suppose, but…."

"Stop the elevator, Joe, and let's go back down. We can find a pastor in town. How about yours?"

"We'll need a licence."

"We can get a licence later. We need only swear to our spiritual commitment before God. That's the main thing."

"I don't know if Pastor Bernard will go for that," I said.

"We won't know unless we ask."

Down we went. Leo would have to wait. Grace wanted to get hitched now, and, as fore me, I had waited my whole life for such a time as this. There was no going back now.

"Phone him, Joe, phone him now," Grace said.

"The signal booster is weak in the elevator. Let's call from my car."

Once we were out on the city's busy streets, I called the church. Pastor Bernard was in.

"It's Joe, Joe LaFlam," I said. "We have an unusual request. Grace and I were wondering if you would marry us. We don't have a license, but we thought we could get that later. We would like you to perform the spiritual part of our commitment, and that way we could become man and wife right away. In other words, we're eloping and we are asking you for your help."

"Hmmm, this isn't Las Vegas," Pastor Bernard said. "It's a highly unusual request, but not unheard of. So you sound like you want to do this right now today."

"That's right," Grace said. "Will you do it? We

need to escape from the cares of this world and from the trials of the PI business and from the stress of having on our shoulders the saving of the human race from demonic servitude.

"Are you sure you shouldn't wait, and perhaps do some pre-marital counselling? It might help you to avert any trouble that might be lurking."

"We're sure," I said.

"Right, well, come on over and we'll see what we can do," Pastor Bernard said.

"Oh, thank you," Grace said. "You won't regret this."

I beeped off Pastor Bernard and felt a sense of relief. The decision had been made. I was in charge of my life. But my self-congratulations were interrupted by my beeping mobile. A familiar voice wanted to know if the elevator had broken down.

"There's been a delay," I said. "We've got other plans."

I beeped off Leo before he could continue expressing his displeasure.

"Look out, Joe, that woman pushing the baby carriage is about to...."

"She shouldn't be out in this weather," I said.

Grace loosed her seatbelt and snuggled closer. The remaining trip to the church was uneventful.

The church main door was open, and Pastor Bernard came out of his office to greet us. He had prepared for our arrival and directed us into the sanctuary where his prophetic elder smiled and said he would be happy to be our witness. I wasn't so sure about that, but beggars couldn't be choosers. The ceremony was short and sweet. We said our repeat-after-me vows, and I kissed the bride. I was glad I had waited until we were wed. She was worth waiting for. Then the prophetic elder had a closing word for us:

A couple were hell bent on marriage
But coupling should never be harried
Life can come fast
But then will it last
Until they are both dead and buried

I appreciated his sentiment, but was reluctant to pay him for his witnessing services. We thanked Pastor Bernard, slipped him his honorarium, and assured him we would get a license as soon as possible. Grace was anxious to get going, and so was I. Life had just taken a wonderful turn. I was now solidly entrenched in my identity. No more transition fragmentation. I had grown. I was now the literate detective, the married literate detective, except for some minor spelling and grammar challenges. But Grace and I would work those out. She was the best partner a man could have. She was literate too and was not shy in correcting me. The world was our oyster.

Pastor Bernard waved to us from the church door, as we climbed into my Bentley.

"Well, where to?" I said.

"Should we go back to your penthouse?" Grace said. "That gruff man should be gone by now and we could get ready to go on our honeymoon."

"Yes, let's do that. I can pack a bag, but what

about you?"

"I don't want to go back home. I can pick up a few things on the way, and then buy whatever I need, wherever we go. I'll phone them with the news from where we end up. Besides, I'm not too happy with their recent treatment of me regarding employment."

"Okay, we're all set then, except for deciding where we should go."

"In the meantime, I don't think there will be any rush once we get to your penthouse, will there? Pen will be gone by now, won't she? And Abner and Alfred would be gone, too."

Grace winked at me. It was the best wink I'd ever received.

CHAPTER THIRTY-ONE

I was in a rush. The sleet had stopped. Grace snuggled ever closer to me now. I shut off my mobile. There would be no interruptions on our way to marital bliss. The streets were as happy as I'd ever seen them. Post Christmas shoppers pranced gaily down the streets and the motorists tipped their hats or smiled broadly as we passed. The sun in collusion with our joy peeked out from behind a cloud, before turning in for the night.

"This is the best ever," Grace said.

"No, it doesn't get any better than this," I said.

"Yes, it will," she said. "Just you wait."

I'd waited my whole life for this. There would be no turning back from happiness now. The die had been cast, the game had been won, and I was the victor at last.

On the way to my penthouse we stopped at a mall, where Grace went in to buy a few things.

"I'll be back in a few minutes. Keep your motor running," she said and then winked.

She returned about a half-hour later carrying a bag and a few boxes. We stowed them in the trunk and then off we went again. We arrived at my building and turned into the parking garage, barely avoiding a collision with a mobile TV unit. We grabbed the packages out of the trunk and juggled them into the elevator. We were almost there. I could feel the excitement of honeymoon heaven rising as we ascended. I would leave the packages at the door, so I could perform the manly, romantic action of carrying her over the threshold. And that's exactly what I did, stumbling in but maintaining my grip on Grace. My penthouse was dark. No Leo, no Pen. We were alone at last. I flicked on the lights. The scene staggered me, but I managed to hold onto Grace. Setting her down, I wanted to know why my office was filled with people. People I knew. People I'd been in contact with over the past week. There was Ralph, aka Polly, and Bill, aka Deep Blue, and Detectives Bannon and Smart, and Leo, and Victor, and the General, and the Admiral, and the hotel clerk, and Darla, and the Lucky Lucy's gang, and who was that guy in the director's chair, who sprang forward to welcome me into my own office and to exclaim that I had been the star of Part Two of Joe LaFlam, PI, on Super Dupers. They gave me a standing ovation. I wasn't thrilled.

In the corner sat Abner and Alfred.

"Well, ya done it again," Abner said. "We warned ya, and ya made a fool of yerself and us, draggin' us into a fake kidnappin' and havin' us guard some hell hole."

"Do you have anything to say to the viewers at home," the director said.

I wasn't going to let them see me defeated. No, I had grown. There was no denying that, and my experience could not be negated by their trickery.

They were the ones who were dealing in deception, not me. I had acted honourably on all counts. Yes, there was no denying that.

"Yes, I would," I said. "I do appreciate all the attention I have received over the past week or so, and even though the case was primarily for entertainment purposes, I hope the viewers have learned a thing or two about the intricacies of detective work. Also, I congratulate you on your skilful directorial skills and, of course, for what I expect will be your stellar camerawork. "

"Thank you," the director said. "You have been the most popular reality star that we have ever had on our show."

"I'm flattered," I said. "Now do you mind shutting off the camera. I need to have a word with Grace."

I asked Grace if she would mind joining me in the bedroom for a short discussion. She was happy to comply. Once behind closed doors, I swallowed the lump in my throat and asked the question.

"What was your part in all this?" I said. "And I do mean your part."

"Oh, Joe, I always wanted to be an actress, and my daddy paid for lessons, and then he pulled some strings to get me on the show. And I think they enjoyed trying their hand at acting, too. Though I don't think they'll appreciate some of Abner's remarks about their business ventures. But then again, with a little pressure from my dad they could be edited out."

"Was Pastor Bernard in on this, too?"

"Yes, he was reluctant at first, but when the show's producer told him the exposure would be good for his church, he agreed. Then on further thought he realized the show would also be a good way to spread the gospel, since Super Dupers reaches millions."

"Okay, so here's the question. Are we married or not?"

"Oh, yes, Joe. There's no doubt about that. Your simplicity captured my heart over and over again. I love your kind heart, Joe."

"That would mean our marriage commitment is genuine."

"Of course, Joe. I wouldn't play around with such a sacred commitment. Our hearts have been united, and we have become one flesh before God. That is if you still want me after I deceived you. But I didn't deceive you about the most important thing."

So all was not lost. In fact everything that counted had been gained. And what I had been most concerned about was no longer an issue. I realized now that she was only acting ditzy for her part in the show. She was a solid human being, and I had struck it rich.

"No, I'm not concerned about that," I said. "You're forgiven. Now let's get that crowd out of here."

We rejoined the cast, who were engaged in self-satisfied conversations about their parts in the show. Alfred and Abner were still sulking in the corner.

"Okay, that's a wrap," the director said. "We captured that final shot in the bedroom. A perfect scene. Thank you, Joe and Grace, for a heart-warming ending to a wonderful instalment of Super Dupers."

"About the money?" Grace said. "You will remember to return our money?"

"We'll be working on that. There are a few legalities we need to address. But I'm sure we'll be successful in retrieving your generous contribution to the show."

"We will be eager to hear from you soon then?" Grace said.

"Okay," the director said. "We will now get out of here and let you kids have some privacy. And don't forget to watch the show you two. That is, if you can take the time on your honeymoon."

I was thankful for his thoughtfulness in quickly clearing out his crew. And I didn't think there was any sense now in being vindictive and suing the show for their felonious use of the knock-out dust. After all, the show must go on. He and the crew vacated, each one giving me a nod of appreciation as they left. I was in no mood to engage any of them in conversation.

"Well, that's that," Alfred said.

"Yes, that is definitely that," Abner agreed.

"I'm sorry you were put through this embarrassment again," I said.

"No problem, you're forgiven," they both said.

"We've been thinking it over," Alfred said.

"Yeah, we been thinkin' it over," Abner said.

"It's time for us to retire," Alfred said. "And since you have given us such a generous retirement package in our contract, we won't have any financial worries. What do you say Abner?"

"Yeah, okay, that's right, you've been more than generous. I'll give ya that. I won't end up back on the street, beggin' for my supper."

"You're welcome," I said. "You deserve to take life easy now after all you have been through over the years."

"Ya, don't worry about us. Just cause the powers that be 'er fixin' to eliminate the seniors by tyin' in euthanasia with their eugenics program to get rid of the older folks who 'er just takin' up space."

"Really, Abner, is that altogether necessary?" Alfred said.

"I'm sorry to hear you're hanging it up," I said. "We've been a good team while it lasted."

"Yes we have, but it looks like you've got a new partner, anyway," Alfred said. "And a partner in more ways than one."

"Don't do this on my account," Grace said. "I would not want that."

"No, our instincts are getting too rusty for the job," Alfred said. "It's not because of you, Grace. Besides, this isn't goodbye. We'll see you in church."

"Ya," Abner said. "And we'll always have homegroup."

"Like I said, I'm sorry to see you go," I said.

"I think our former boss is hintin' that we leave now," Abner said.

"Let's go, Abner, there's no sense dragging this out any longer."

We shook hands, and Grace thanked them

both and kissed them goodbye. As they left, I had conflicting emotions. The immediate ones concerning my new bride won out. We were together now, and nothing would separate us except death.

My cell rang.

"Don't answer it, Joe," Grace said.

"What's the harm?" I said.

I beeped it on speaker phone. A snaky voice hissed in a southern drawl.

"You don't think this is over, do you, Laflam?"

"Hang up," Grace said.

"You haven't seen trouble yet, LaFlam," the voice said. "And that goes for you too, little gal."

"Okay, who is this?" I said. "I'm sure you're aware that we're not available right now for Super Dupers part three."

"You've got that wrong, LaFlam. Spelunkers Global is on the move, and we're going to take the whole system down and you with it."

"Is there some reason you insist on including me in your plans?" I said. "Why don't you just go back into your hole and feed your pet gopher."

"Not that you deserve an answer, LaFlam, but we like to include you in our plans because you're always sticking your nose in where it doesn't belong. Super Dupers is only a warm up. We're going to teach you a lesson, a deadly lesson, one you'll never forget."

"Nobody ever dies in my cases," I said. "And besides, how could I remember the lesson if I'm dead,"

"You've got him there, Joe," Grace said. "Excellent reasoning."

"Alright, that's all for now," he said. "But you'll be hearing from us. And just so you know, we're going to take down the real Alliance, and the real Q, and especially the real Q+, and we are going to annihilate all that you call holy in your self-righteous world."

"I've heard this all before. We're not interested in your game, whatever it is."

I beeped him off.

"Well done, Joe, we don't have to put up with his sort anymore. But if they do need to be dealt with, we'll be here to deal with them, won't we, Joe."

"That's the spirit, partner. You're getting the hang of this business already. LaFlam & LaFlam, sounds great doesn't it?

"You mean, LaFlam & Lane, don't you, Joe?"

"Right, what was I thinking? Either way we'll be unbeatable. Of course you'll need some instruction to acquaint yourself with the PI business, and you'll need to get a license, and whatever else, but we are now set for life and all that the future might hold."

Yes, I was the literate detective now, and my foundation was solid. I knew who I was and what my purpose in the world was meant to be. And I was well mated.

"I do have a question to ask you, Joe. And remember you can be honest with me and you're safe to tell me anything."

"Shoot, I'll do my best to give you a straight answer."

"Well, here goes. Did you know it was all a setup from the beginning? Did you really believe all of that

Deep Blue and Polly stuff?"

"Sure, I suspected all along there was something fishy going on. But at the same time I was on a mission to see how deep the enemy would take us."

"Of course, Joe, I thought so. You outsmarted us all."

My answer was sort of the truth. I kind of had my suspicions all along. But my main goal was achieved. I might not have succeeded in defeating the Spelunkers, but I got myself a wife.

"I do wonder," I said, "how much you were acting and how much you were being honest with me."

"We're all actors in a way, Joe."

Ahh, so I married a deep thinker. We were two of a kind. This was the stuff that dreams were made of.

And one thing for certain, the devil was still down there, or up there, or through there, or wherever your theology might place him. The battle was not over. In fact, it was just beginning. And until the Lord came back to finish the job, we would be here, Grace and I, to confront the enemy wherever and whenever he exposed his evil head. But not until after our extended honeymoon, of course. Yes, this wasn't the end. It was only the beginning.

"We have long road ahead of us," I said. "And we are going to succeed in our mission to save the world from those Spelunkers scum."

"Oh, Joe, you're the greatest," Grace said, and winked the kind of wink that could only mean one thing.

The End

BOOKS BY THIS AUTHOR

Confessions Of A Charismatic Christian

The Charismatic Movement came and went. Rick Dewhurst experienced most of it, dating back to 1980. From John Wimber's Vineyard Church in Anaheim, to the Kansas City prophets, to Rick Joyner's MorningStar Ministries, to the Toronto Blessing, he was there to see it all. This is his memoir, focusing on the spiritual highlights of his 40-year journey.

The Dregs Of Aquarius

Fresh, insightful, and often hilarious, The Dregs of Aquarius is a counter-culture Catcher in the Rye that speaks to the generation coming of age now, as well as to those Baby Boomers who can't remember much about the whole scene and might want a refresher. And for those who might simply want to get away to another time and place that is authentically portrayed, The Dregs of Aquarius is the perfect trip.

The Darkest Valley

In the Cowichan Valley on beautiful Vancouver Island, a pastor's wife with a deep secret is dying of cancer, his young aboriginal convert is in danger of being grabbed and initiated into brutal Longhouse spirit dancing rituals, and his congregation is throwing him to the wolves. In desperation, he attempts to recruit a local newspaper editor to publish the truth about the Longhouse. Along the way truth is put to the test, and when his wife's secret is revealed, so is their faith.

The Good Book Club

PI Jane Sunday investigates the murder of the associate pastor of a church gone wrong. A solid jolt of detective fiction, The Good Book Club compels lovers of the genre to hold on tight to the emotional roller-coaster until the very end.

My Fear Lady

Gumshoe Joe LaFlam again goes head-to-head with Spelunkers Global, this time going undercover underground to bust the conspirators. And also get the girl.

Bye Bye Bertie

Investigating a kidnapping case, gumshoe Joe LaFlam

runs afoul of Spelunkers Global, a secret society bent on world domination. Joe undertakes a desperate 21-day fast to twist God's arm to help him solve the case, make some good money, and get the girl, any girl.

www.ingramcontent.com/pod-product-compliance
Lightning Source LLC
Chambersburg PA
CBHW071238260626
47159CB00005BA/1791